"Please, Brody." Callie wrung her hands. "Help her."

"Why not have your fancy trainers look at her?"

Callie winced. "They can't know she's blind. My sponsors gave me six weeks to get her back in running condition. If we're not back by the end of summer, then I lose my sponsorships."

"What does her being blind have to do with anything?"

"It makes her a liability. I'm willing to take the risk, but a blind horse running barrels? Come on, you know they'll never go for it."

Brody crossed his arms. "What do your sponsors say about you taking her off the circuit for six weeks when she's been declared fit?"

Callie paused. "They know Glow is struggling to get back into running the pattern. I just... neglected to tell them about the blindness."

"Callie—"

"They'll make me run without her. I made a promise when we left that it was me and her until the end."

"You're good at breaking promises. I'm sure Glow won't hold it against you." Unlike him.

Tabitha Bouldin has a bachelor's degree in creative writing/English from Southern New Hampshire University. She is a member of American Christian Fiction Writers (ACFW) and an avid reader when her three cats will allow her to pick up a book. Living in Tennessee her entire life, Tabitha grew up riding horses and adopting every stray animal she could find.

Books by Tabitha Bouldin

The Cowgirl's Last Rodeo

Visit the Author Profile page at LoveInspired.com.

The Cowgirl's
Last Rodeo

Tabitha Bouldin

LOVE INSPIRED
INSPIRATIONAL ROMANCE

LOVE INSPIRED®
INSPIRATIONAL ROMANCE

ISBN-13: 978-1-335-59707-6

The Cowgirl's Last Rodeo

Recycling programs
for this product may
not exist in your area.

Love Inspired
22 Adelaide St. West, 41st Floor
Toronto, Ontario M5H 4E3, Canada
www.LoveInspired.com

Printed in U.S.A.

For we walk by faith, not by sight.
    —*2 Corinthians* 5:7

I could not do this without the unwavering support of my family. I love you all. Thank you for standing by me.

To God be the glory for giving me the stories that live rent-free in my head at all hours of the day...and night.

Chapter One

Brody Jacobs planted his boots on the worn linoleum. "It's not that bad, Mom."

Mom crossed from the stove, her spatula dripping bacon grease onto the floor, and placed a piece of paper on the scarred table. Brody's shoulders drooped as he traced the lines of numbers marching down the overdue bill in neat columns. He tapped the final row and glanced up in time to see Mom's mouth pinch.

His insides heaved.

They both knew the truth but neither gave voice to the reality staring them down in black ink. The Triple Bar Ranch was going belly-up and, with Dad's medical bills... Brody flattened his hand over the dreaded red stamp. He'd done his best and cowboyed up after Dad's accident ten years ago. Taking over the ranch and turning it into a training facility for horses had been his best option, and the reason he'd stayed behind in Tamarack Springs—their quaint little town in the foothills of North Carolina's Blue Ridge Mountains—instead of following his dreams. He'd managed to keep the ranch afloat until the latest doctor's appointment had revealed his father needed yet another surgery. They hadn't even paid off the last one.

"How's Dad?" Brody ran a hand through his hair. Curls fell around his ears. He needed a haircut, but there'd been no time in the last month to drive into town and waste time on something that his Stetson covered.

Mom's chin quivered. She shook her head and went back to flipping the bacon. "Cranky. Why don't you go see him while I finish breakfast?"

"I'm fine." Dad rolled his wheelchair into the kitchen and propped his elbows on the padded armrests. "How's that new mare?" He aimed the question at Brody while rubbing a gnarled hand across his gray whiskers.

Brody shuffled toward the door. "Settling in. Nice gait. She'll make a good trail horse once she stops being afraid of her own shadow." He snatched a handful of bacon from the platter as Mom carried it past. "I'm headed to the barn." He shoved a piece into his mouth and hurried outside.

The porch steps shuddered under his heavy tread. Grass crunched under his heels. In the distance, the barn loomed, a dark spectacle against the rising sun. A horse whinnied from the pasture across the driveway. A tawny head with a salt-and-pepper mane hung over the split rail and nuzzled Brody's neck when he stepped closer to the fence. Brody patted the gelding. "Breakfast in an hour." He drew in a breath of oak, dew-laden grass and the coffee he cradled in his other hand.

The gelding snuffled his palm then ambled away when he found nothing but the lingering scent of bacon.

Molly, his youngest sister, emerged from her cabin on the other side of the half-acre yard, her four-year-old son in tow. She tossed a wave Brody's way and he answered with a lift of his chin.

He entered the barn and flicked a switch, sending a wash of light across the concrete aisle. Several horses complained with snorts and stamping hooves, but soon they leaned across their half doors and bobbed their heads at him. Brody inhaled deeply, breathing in the aromas of equine, dirt, manure, molasses and leather. A home-brewed concoction that plunged into his heart. Home. He'd once dreamed of leaving. A long time ago. Before Dad's accident had rendered him a paraplegic and sent the family into a frenzy of financial woes.

Grabbing a lead rope, Brody moved to the Appaloosa pacing her stall. "Let's go, Missy." The mare spun at the sound of her name and reached over to bump Brody with her nose. He clipped the lead onto her halter and led the mare to the round pen.

Wooden slats made up the pen and ensured the horses he worked with had little to no distractions. He removed the lead and moved his hand in a circle. They'd worked on this command for weeks. Missy tossed her head and broke into a slow trot. "Atta girl." The mare snorted and bobbed her head, the equivalent of a horse's "thank you for noticing." He chuckled and followed the mare's movement.

Gravel crunched from the driveway. Brody tipped his Stetson up to get a better look at the horse trailer rumbling toward the barn. The mare skidded to a halt now that he wasn't watching and turned her head in his direction. Brody didn't move as he took in the truck's details. He wasn't expecting company, but a trailer spoke of someone possibly needing a horse trained.

Training meant cash. Cash meant relief.

Dirt lined the truck's lower half but couldn't take away the dollar signs he knew came attached to a rig that size. The trailer alone was worth more than his two-bedroom house. Whoever drove had it well in hand, hauling the white gooseneck right up to his weathered barn. He caught sight of a single horse through the trailer windows. Who used a six-stall gooseneck to haul one horse?

Brody shook his head and slipped through the gate. One way to find out. If Mr. Fancy Pants wanted training, Brody would do well to put his best boot forward. His shoulders tightened as he forced out a smile that most likely made him look like a gargoyle. Grit dug into his cheeks. Couldn't be helped after working in the corral. Dirt came with the territory. And sweat. He swiped a hand over his brow before tugging his hat back in place.

The driver's-side door swung open. Brody snapped his gaze upward as he approached the truck and locked eyes with the blue-eyed beauty he'd not seen in ten years.

Callie. He choked on her name and swallowed to dislodge the boulder taking up residence in his throat.

"Hello, Brody." A pair of battered, charcoal boots hit the ground with a soft *thump* and Callie staggered a step.

Brody caught her elbow and then flinched back when the contact brought memories rushing in with overwhelming force. After all these years, he'd hoped and prayed to leave those feelings behind. No such happenings. Not for him.

Callie righted herself and offered her rodeo smile, the one that showed her teeth and carved dimples into her cheeks. That smile told him more than he cared to know. Either she was scared, or she thought she'd put on a show. He knocked his heel on the ground and ran his thumbs into his belt loops while making certain his face betrayed nothing of the lingering echo of feelings from their past.

"What are you doing back in Tamarack Springs?" His voice came out hoarse, the tone accusatory.

Callie's smile faded. She huffed a dark laugh and a streak of weariness flashed through her eyes. "I need your help."

His stampeding heart lurched to a halt before the drumming resumed at a slower pace. Of course she did. The great Callie Wade wouldn't set foot back in her small hometown unless driven by the whip. Or her sponsors.

He narrowed his eyes and took another look at the truck, making certain she was truly alone.

Their last night together sprang up in his mind. His proposal. Her rejection. The fight that led to her stomping off and riding out of town without a goodbye, leaving a ten-year silence in her wake.

He supposed her career had had a lot to do with that. She'd been adamant that the rodeo circuit was the place where she'd find happiness. Barrel racing had been her dream as long as his had been horse training.

That was before she'd gone without him, choosing a stranger, who'd promised her all the big sponsors and more money than she ever dreamed possible, over him. She and Samantha Blade had made headlines. Famous rodeo queens who ran the barrels fast enough to blow the dirt right off his boots.

While he'd been here, training horses for pennies on the dollar.

"I'm busy." He spun on his bootheel and waved a hand over his shoulder. "Try again in another ten years."

Callie ran after him, jumped in front of him to cut him off, her hands landing on his shoulders. With their faces inches from each other and tears gathered on her lashes, her voice shuddered as she said, "Glow's blind."

Those two words hit him with a one-two punch and sent him reeling. Brody slammed a palm to the corral fence. Without that support, he'd have crumpled to the ground as pain lanced his heart. Glow. Golden Glow, as she was known in the arena, but Glow to him and Callie. They'd raised the mare together, Brody teaching the horse to run and Callie riding with a fierceness that gave her the nickname Calamity Jane.

"How?" Countless questions raced through his mind but he locked onto that one and let it fall.

Callie's shoulders lifted to her ears and her hands fell to her sides. She tucked them into her pockets, leaving the knuckles exposed. It was such a Callie move that he almost missed the scar running across her wrist. When had that happened?

He clenched his hands to keep them steady.

Her eyes went soft as she scanned the trailer then cold when she moved to him. "Hereditary disease." She stopped and swallowed. "We didn't know anything was wrong until she went down in Texas. Sprained a tendon in her foreleg and the vet did a full workup. She had some sight then, but that's gone."

A shrill whinny burst from the trailer. The mare in the arena answered, nostrils quivering as she paced the side closest to the trailer.

"I can't cure blindness, Callie." He reached for the lead rope wrapped around the top rail and folded it into his hands, more for something to do than because he needed it. The mare would follow him to the barn with or without it. "And a sprained tendon is something you know how to treat. I'm a trainer, not a vet."

"She won't run anymore." Callie's voice quivered. "Every time I get in the saddle, she stands there like a statue. Won't move at all."

Brody buffed the back of his neck. "If she's lost heart, there's nothing I can do."

"Please, Brody." Callie wrung her hands, twisting her fingers into a knot. "I'm desperate. Help her."

Dollar signs swam through his head. How much could he ask for payment? Callie probably made good money in the rodeo. She drove a fancy rig and most likely had all sorts of people at her beck and call. That brought up a question. "Why me?" He angled his head until the hat's brim shaded his eyes and observed Callie from the shadows. "Why not have your fancy trainers look at her?"

Callie winced and huffed out a sigh that sounded like regret. "They can't know she's blind. You trained that blind gelding when we were kids. I know you can train Glow." She waited a beat then moved to the rear of the trailer and started to undo the latch. Same old Callie. Moving forward before he had a chance to say anything. "My sponsors gave me six weeks to get her back in running condition, starting today. She's already been off the circuit for a month to heal the sprain. We need to be back by the end of summer."

"What does her being blind have to do with anything?"

"It makes her a liability. I'm willing to take the risk, but a blind horse running barrels? Come on, you know they'll never go for it. Only animals in peak condition are considered for the 1D."

The 1D. The horses with the fastest times were put into the 1D bracket, a place where Callie and Glow excelled.

Brody crossed his arms. "What do your sponsors say about you taking her off the circuit for six weeks when she's been declared fit?"

Callie paused, her hands gripping the trailer latch. A quick glance at him revealed a sliver of guilt. "We crashed in Texas. Took out the third barrel. They know Glow is struggling to get back into running the pattern."

"You're lying to them?" Unbelievable. He jerked his Stetson from his head and whacked it on his thigh.

She shook her head vehemently, sending her blond braid flying over her shoulder. "It's true she's having trouble. I just…neglected to tell them about the blindness."

"Callie—"

"They'll make me run without her." Callie spun the latch open and swung the trailer door, exposing the interior to a bloom of sunlight that caught Glow's coat. The golden palomino shifted her hooves but didn't move more than a step. Her nose skimmed the trailer's side, staying in constant contact. "I made a promise when we left that it was me and her until the end."

"You're good at breaking promises. I'm sure Glow won't hold it against you." Unlike him. Pain shifted his insides, working through his heart and sending a pounding tempo into his temples. She'd made promises to Brody. Promises that she'd broken without a look back or even a goodbye. "I can't help you."

Glow whickered at the sound of his voice and her golden ears swiveled in his direction.

Brody closed his eyes against the flood of emotion.

When he opened them, Glow had turned her head to face him.

"I'm sorry," Callie said. "If it was any other horse, I'd back down. But it isn't. It's Glow, and I can't do this without her."

But she could do it without him. Ten years proved that she hadn't needed him for anything. Not until now.

Glow shifted and grunted out a sigh.

He was going to regret this. Brody stepped into the trailer and dropped his voice to a whisper. "Hey, girl." He didn't touch Glow. Not yet. He took another step, letting his boots rattle the hay and warn Glow of his approach. He grumbled a low monologue with each step. Glow's ears followed him until he reached her side.

Brody held out his hand, palm up, near the mare's nostrils. She breathed him in and then moved her nose until it rested against his wrist. She relaxed, the tense and quivering muscles smoothing out as a heavy snuffle warmed his arm. He patted her neck and stroked down to her shoulder, then repeated the motion, talking all the while.

Finally, he stepped back and faced Callie, who stood outside the trailer with a look in her eyes that he couldn't decipher. "Bring her to the round pen. Let me get a good look at her."

Callie moved to embrace him as he stepped down from the trailer. Brody jerked away before he did something foolish and glared until Callie stepped back. "I'm doing this for Glow. No promises. She may never run again. You need to be prepared for that."

"But imagine if she does." Callie folded her arms across her stomach and hugged her ribs. "Once she wins, I don't care who knows she's blind. You'll be touted as the best trainer in the south. You'll be famous."

Famous. Callie's words kept landing blows. He recovered from one in time for another to kick his legs out from under him. He'd wanted to be famous. To live a life in the spotlight and have everyone clamoring at his door, begging for his help in training their horses.

Childhood dreams that were denied reality. He'd made do on his own, training show horses and helping riders learn how to communicate with their mounts.

"I'll send you a bill." He trudged to the corral and led the Appaloosa mare to the barn.

If there was prize money to be won on the longest run of mistakes, Callie had it in the bag. She ran her hands along Glow's withers and forced down the tears threatening to choke her. "I'm sorry, Glow."

Glow snorted and shook her head. Milky eyes rolled. Callie struggled to believe it and even now had to force the word out. Blind. The horse that encompassed her hopes and dreams, and her past with Brody, whuffled Callie's arm and leaned into the hand on her side. "We'll make it better. Brody will make you better."

Callie had to believe that. Had to trust that the man she'd left behind would step up and help the mare they both loved. She needed him to do this. Without Glow, she had almost zero chance of winning. Her sponsors had offered her another horse, a young gelding named Maverick, who took to the barrels with an enthusiasm that left his riders breathless.

But he wasn't Glow.

She'd started this journey with Glow, and she wanted one more race. The accident that had revealed Glow's blindness could not be their end. Callie refused to allow that to be their final moments under the rodeo lights.

Glow deserved the chance to become a champion before Sam decided Glow was too much of a risk and sold her.

Callie gulped back tears. Under no circumstances could Brody learn that Callie had sold Glow. She still owned partial shares, but Samantha held the majority, and if she found out about Glow's blindness, the mare would be at the next auction before Callie could un-hitch the trailer. Sam didn't believe in keeping horses that couldn't make money. It wouldn't matter that Callie wanted to raise foals from Glow. Samantha worked in pragmatisms and wouldn't want foals from a mare with a known degenerative disease. She'd cut her losses. Callie had tried to buy Glow back over the years, but there was never enough money, and there wouldn't be until she landed some major wins. Her sponsors were the ones helping her keep up appearances.

She'd promised to pay Brody, and she'd uphold her end of the bargain. But between rodeo fees, Glow's reg-ular upkeep and a recent streak of losses that ate into her savings, her finances were floundering. She didn't even own the truck and trailer she drove. The last four weeks of not being able to compete, combined with the upcoming six weeks without a job or rodeos that would bring in money, were a serious drain. If things didn't change, she'd be forced to dip into the funds she'd set aside for buying Glow back from Sam.

Brody's voice reached her from outside the trailer. "Ev-erything okay?" His voice had a huskiness to it, a deepness that hadn't been present before. Ten years had changed him, matured him. Lines fanned out from his eyes, eyes that seemed to peer into her with a depth and clarity that made keeping secrets almost impossible.

Callie ran her hand along Glow's jaw and took the lead in her palm. She clucked her tongue. "Let's go, girl."

Glow followed Callie with hesitant steps. She paused after each hoof struck and tucked her nose into Callie's back.

Her eyes burned with unshed tears. Why Glow? *God, why?*

"Wait." Brody blocked her exit from the trailer. He gripped his belt and tilted his head to the side. "Did she give you any trouble walking into the trailer?"

Callie chewed her cheek but nodded. No sense in lying to the man about Glow's condition.

"I want you to move to the edge of the trailer but don't step down."

Callie did as instructed.

Glow shook and her steps shortened.

"Easy, Glow." Brody nodded at Callie. "Rap your knuckles on the frame on either side of you. Let her hear it, then step down. Let her feel you move. We need to start teaching her words or sounds to associate with the movement that is coming next." Brody tapped his hands on the metal on either side of Callie with a resounding *ping*.

Glow took another step, her whiskers tickling the back of Callie's neck. She started to move the mare away, but Brody shook his head. "Let her stay there so she can feel your movement. You're her eyes now. Tell her to step down and then you move. Word then action."

"Step down." Callie's voice shook as she followed Brody's directions. She moved along the ramp, her steps loud.

Glow hesitated.

Brody rapped the trailer frame again and Glow moved

her nose to touch the metal. "I'm showing her the path by letting her hear the obstacles." Once the mare felt the metal, she took the first step onto the ramp and lifted her head to scent the air. "Good. Now keep her walking. Let her loosen up a bit."

The smooth timbre of Brody's voice relaxed the knot in Callie's middle. The knot she'd carried since the vet's announcement four weeks ago. Every step forward helped ease the tension. Callie let out a breath that Glow mimicked. Her steps quickened until they reached the round pen.

Brody jogged ahead and opened the gate. "This is wide enough that she shouldn't have any trouble. Any time you get to a narrow gate, show her the space by making noise. Let her take her time."

"What about in the arena? How can I show her the barrels when we're running?"

"One step at a time. This isn't a quick fix. You can't expect her to do things the same just because you want her to. She's learning the world all over again, and she's dependent on you to show her the way." He stepped back and watched as they entered the circle.

Grass turned to sand and Callie's boots sank into the soft ground. She took in the heady air growing thick with summer and lowered her shoulders. Glow nosed Callie's back and she turned to run her hands around the mare's eyes. Glow leaned into the pressure and dropped her head to the sand. "Think I can turn her loose?"

"Walk her around the perimeter first." Brody used his thumb to push his hat away from his eyes. His ice-blue gaze found her and held her captive. Curls peeked from beneath the hat, their length a delightful surprise from the shorn hair she remembered. Whiskers dotted his cheeks, a sure sign he'd not shaved in a day or so. It suited him.

She clenched her hand around the rope. One look from Brody and she was ready to heave every secret into the broad chasm between them and ask him to help her climb out of the void she'd created.

She regretted leaving him. Regretted the fight and her accusations that he didn't love her enough. She'd been a foolish girl back then. A foolish girl who'd thought if she left, he'd follow.

If he had, then Brody would not be the man she knew him to be under the surly tones. A tone he left behind when speaking to Glow. Only then did his eyes warm and his stride turn smooth. His long legs closed the distance between them. He paced ahead of Callie and knocked his knuckles against the wooden planks with every step. He'd scrape all the skin off if he kept that up, but Callie pressed her lips closed.

They were working together for the first time in ten years. Whatever Brody thought best, is what she'd do. He knew horses. They responded to him in a way that showed God's handiwork—a downright gift from above. He'd taught a blind pony to jump when they were thirteen. Those were the reasons she'd come to him. Even if she'd had the most famous trainer at her disposal, she'd have come here…to Brody. To have one last chance to prove herself to her parents. They'd never wanted kids, and her presence proved to be a distraction they could not tolerate.

"Can you get on her bareback?"

Brody's question snapped Callie from her thoughts. They'd made a complete circuit of the pen and Glow hadn't stopped once. Callie arched an eyebrow at Brody in question.

"I want to see her reaction to you on her back. No movement required." When she nodded, he put his back to the rail and propped his elbows on a board, the picture of a relaxed cowboy. "Take her to the center and hop on. I'm assuming you don't need help."

Even if she did, she wouldn't ask him. Letting him boost her onto Glow was out of the question. She lost her footing at the thought. No, sir. She did not need Brody giving her a leg up. She directed Glow to the center, heart slamming her ribs and turning her mouth to cotton. Glow stopped at Callie's gentle "whoa" and planted her hooves.

Callie swallowed and tossed the lead across Glow's withers. The mare twitched her braided tail but otherwise remained still. Callie backed up a step, grabbed a handful of the mare's mane and swung herself onto her broad back.

Glow froze.

Callie breathed in through her nose and out her mouth.

Brody remained in a relaxed position against the railing. He eyed them for a long minute, until Callie's heart drummed in her ears and her vision swam.

He dropped his heel from the lowest board and lifted his chin. "I'll help Glow. On one condition."

Callie's shoulders stiffened and her spine snapped straight. The question she needed to ask pulsed in her throat, unable to move past the blockade.

He murmured reassurances as he ambled to the center of the arena and stopped at Glow's shoulder, running his hand along Glow's neck as he glanced up at Callie.

"We don't talk unless we're training."

Chapter Two

After a long night sleeping in the truck, Callie twisted the cap on her white-chocolate mocha and dropped a handful of change in the mason jar labeled Tips while the customer behind her rattled off a coffee order as long as Callie's arm.

She'd agreed to Brody's request that they not speak unless they were training and then bedded Glow down in an empty stall. With nothing else to do, she'd cruised around town in search of a place to crash for the night.

What would have been easy in any other town proved impossible in her hometown of two thousand occupants.

She rubbed at her gritty eyes and squinted at her surroundings.

Brewsters, the local coffee shop, hadn't changed much in the last ten years. The laminate flooring still had a crack running down the center, the yellow color had faded to butter, and Patrick still made the best coffee Callie had ever tasted.

"Hey, it was good to see you, Callie." A man roughly her age slid a sleeve over another coffee cup and nodded in her direction.

She mimicked the movement and forced her lips into a smile. "You too." Taking a sip of her coffee, Callie moved toward the door and shouldered it open after stepping over the jagged floor. The old nursery rhyme whispered past her defenses. She and Brody used to hold hands and hop over the crack, pretending they were leaping into the future.

"Here, let me get that." A feminine voice rode the summer breeze down Main Street and the door was pulled away from Callie's arm. She looked around at the sharp inhale that ended with her name. "Callie."

"Tenley?" Callie shuffled to the side to keep from blocking the door. Brody's sister stood with her mouth agape. The middle sibling, Tenley, was a born rebel, always getting into trouble and doing what she could to annoy her older brother.

"What are you doing here?" Tenley shook her head and released the door. "Are you back for good?"

A couple buzzed past, chattering about a ballgame starting soon. Callie absorbed the moment of sunshine, fresh coffee and Tamarack Springs—a ripe mixture of chlorine from the local pool and cattle from the surrounding farmland. "Brody didn't tell you?" She'd assumed he'd inform the whole family of her return. Though it had only been a day. Maybe he wanted to break it to them gently.

Tenley winced and jerked one shoulder toward her ear. Callie understood. This brother/sister duo agreed on nothing. Callie had often thought that Tenley argued with Brody for the sake of it. Nothing pleased her more than getting a rise out of her big brother.

"Brody is helping me train."

"Wow. That's…" Tenley trailed off and cleared her

throat. She looked up and caught Callie's gaze. Tension corded Tenley's neck and caused the veins to stand out in stark relief. "That's great."

"Yep." A gulp of coffee sweetened Callie's mood. She toed the sidewalk with her hand-tooled boot and scanned the street. Three cars lined the space in front of Brewsters. Another trundled down the road and backfired as it sputtered to a stop at the end of the block. "You know of any places for rent? I checked at the Langleys', but they've closed the motel for renovations. Larry said they were opening a bed-and-breakfast this fall?"

Tenley's head bobbed and she picked at a nail. "Yes to the B and B. No to the place to rent. Only available lodging is in Bridgeport." Bridgeport. A slightly larger town two hours away.

Callie groaned. The commute would be a pain, but she'd made the commitment to Glow. No way she would back out because of a long drive.

Brody's sister chewed on her lip and put her shoulder to the glass window while folding her arms over her stomach. "Why don't you stay with me? I have a spare room."

"Oh, I couldn't." A gust of relief tightened Callie's hands on the coffee cup. Staying with Tenley solved more than one problem. It saved her time driving back and forth, but more importantly, she'd save money on gas and motels. She needed as much help as she could get. Her resistance came from good, old-fashioned Southern roots. One didn't impose on the goodwill of neighbors. At least, not on the first asking.

Tenley grinned and rolled her eyes, but played along. "You'd be doing me a favor. And I won't charge you as much as the hotels. Come on." She lifted her eyebrows. "It'll be like old times."

Old times. Callie's gut clenched. Summer sleepovers and nights filled with laughter as they chased lightning bugs across open fields and rode their horses on mountain paths before daylight broke the horizon. Hour upon hour spent with the Jacobs siblings thundered past on heavy hooves. A need to have that again cinched her decision.

"When you put it like that, how can I resist?"

"Great." Tenley pushed off from the window. "I'll be back later, but you're welcome to unpack and settle in."

Tenley moved away.

Callie snagged her sleeve. "Hold on. Where do you live now?"

"In the house east of the barn. You remember it, don't you?"

Heart thumping, Callie gripped the coffee cup until her knuckles popped. "You live on the ranch?"

"We all do. Molly took the cabin across the driveway and Brody is in the house by the woods." Tenley's nose scrunched as she took in Callie's expression. "It's a perfect setup. You'll be right there for training and I get a roommate."

"Are you sure Brody won't mind?"

Tenley's snort rivaled Glow's. She jerked the door open and slipped inside while calling over her shoulder, "Brody minds everything. Do it anyway."

Typical Tenley.

Callie chewed her lip as she made her way back to her truck. No way she'd sleep in the cab again tonight. Living the rodeo life had taught her how to survive in tight spaces, how to pack light and how to sleep at the drop of a hat. But she drew the line at living out of the truck for six weeks.

Tenley left Brewsters and hurried across the road, moving toward the small library tucked behind a row of maple trees. Callie resisted the urge to call out and ask a dozen questions. Maybe she'd call around Bridgeport and check out the motels there. A two-hour drive each way had to be better than living under Brody's nose.

Decision made, she started walking while scrolling through her phone. Two motels in Bridgeport, each with online pictures that made her skin crawl. She shuddered and tossed her empty cup in the trash.

She reached the end of the block and turned left, angling onto the dirt path that looped toward the ball field.

The sound of a bat striking a ball cracked the air. Callie lifted her head and eyed the field where what looked like an entire team of T-ball players chased a ball across the grass.

"Luke, you're supposed to run to the base, not chase the ball." Brody's laughter mixed with his words and warmed Callie more than coffee ever could.

She huddled at the edge of the bleachers and tucked her phone in her jeans' pocket. Sweat pooled along her hairline and trickled down her jaw.

Brody removed his ball cap and whacked it against his leg. "Run, Luke." Dressed in a blue T-shirt with Tamarack Tornadoes stamped out in white lettering, he reminded Callie of his dad. An ache settled over her heart. She rubbed at the spot and smiled as the boy who must be Luke zigzagged from first to second base.

In the outfield, a girl picked up the ball and hurtled it toward the pitcher's mound, but there was no one there to catch it.

Luke rounded second, tucked his chin and barreled for third.

A woman in the stands jumped to her feet and started shouting Luke's name.

Callie followed the sound and recognized Molly, Brody's youngest sister, clapping her hands and cheering as Luke slid onto home plate.

"Well, if it isn't Calamity Jane."

Callie tensed at the nickname but dropped her rigid posture when a stooped man in a wheelchair rolled to her side. Emotion clogged her throat. She'd known the accident had been bad, but the wheelchair came as a shock. What else wasn't Brody telling her? "Hello, Mr. Jacobs." She took his outstretched hand and gave it a shake while covering her shock. Calluses scuffed her palm. Lifting her gaze, Callie met Brody's mother's stare and swallowed hard enough to make her throat ache. "Mrs. Jacobs."

"Pish." Mr. Jacobs waved his hand. Leathery skin spiderwebbed with blue veins flashed in the sunlight. "I think we're past all that, don't you? Last I remember, you called us Peter and Margaret."

An urge to apologize seized Callie. What was it about this place that made her feel like a little girl again? She'd turn thirty soon, but looking at Brody's parents shaved off the last ten years like they'd never existed.

"Brody tells us he's helping you with Glow." Margaret gripped the wheelchair's handles and leaned forward. Warmth radiated from her eyes and her smile appeared genuine. "I remember when that horse was born. You two were over the moon."

Callie relaxed when they didn't ask what happened to Glow or why she'd come home. Home. "She's a great horse. I wouldn't be this close to a championship without her." Winning a rodeo here and there was nice, but not what she'd left home for. She wanted the title of world champion. The rest remained unsaid but burned hotter than a brand on the edge of her tongue. Glow needed a comeback. Callie needed the winnings to buy back Samantha's shares. Life as a professional cowgirl came with long days and little pay, at least in the beginning—before she'd made a name for herself. With no one to help her in those early years, she'd sold her shares of Glow to stay in the rodeo. A mistake she sorely regretted.

"Have you found a place to stay?" Peter laced his fingers together over his lap and peered up at Callie.

It was just like him to read her mind.

Brody's voice called out from the game, ushering his team onto the field. Conversations flowed from the bleachers, the general hub of noise a steady constant that Callie latched onto while forcing her voice to remain steady. "Tenley offered to let me stay with her, but I'm looking into the motels in Bridgeport."

"Oh, no. That won't do." Margaret's brown curls waved as she wagged her head side to side. "Bedbugs and creeps. That's what you'll find in Bridgeport. No. You'll stay with Tenley." She said it with the kind but forceful tone of a mother who brooked no argument. Margaret Jacobs said her piece and her word was final.

Their easy acceptance rocked Callie onto her heels. She'd expected some fallout from her leaving. Instead, they welcomed her. Everyone except Brody.

"I don't want to be in the way."

"You all but lived with us before, Callie. Makes no difference now." Peter eyed her, his blue eyes warm and friendly.

How many hours had Callie spent at their home during her younger years? The Jacobs siblings had always said they'd build houses right there on the family ranch, and they'd followed through. Back then, Callie was one of the crew. She should feel like an outsider now, but the Jacobses' hospitality chased those emotions away.

"Well, if I'm moving in, I might as well head over." Callie pushed off from the bleachers and tucked her fingertips into her pockets. "I'd like to check in on Glow."

"Make yourself at home." Margaret reached down and squeezed Peter's shoulder. "We'll be along after Luke's game, but the house is unlocked if you need anything."

Only in Tamarack Springs could a house be left unlocked and the homeowners come back to not a single thing missing. She'd never known any of the Jacobses to lock a door.

"Dinner at six." Margaret's voice followed Callie.

She bit back a grin. Another order from Brody's mother.

Dirt puffed beneath Brody's boots. He hauled the duffel bag from the back of the truck and tossed it onto his porch before making his way down to the barn. Darkness descended when he stepped inside and he blinked to clear his vision.

Murmured voices carried from the back stall. No. Voice, singular. Callie's voice. Brody halted in surprise when he found her with Glow.

Callie's crooning stopped abruptly.

Glow stood in the middle of the stall with her head under Callie's arm. Callie stroked the mare's face, fingertips drifting over the mare's closed eyes and tangling in the flaxen mane.

"Do you need something, Brody?" Her voice was soft, and it took him a minute to realize she'd spoken to him and not the horse.

He shook his head and stepped back. "No. Just heard you talking and wanted to check on Glow. You want to work today?" He faced the barn doors to keep from seeing the pain in Callie's eyes as she glanced up at him. Seeing Glow like this burrowed deep inside and squeezed until he felt like an overjuiced orange.

"Let her rest today. It was a long drive from Texas." Callie shifted in the straw and eased her arm from around Glow's neck. The mare snorted. Callie murmured to Glow the entire time. Once Callie moved to the door, the horse raised her head and shuffled forward. Callie gave the mare one last pat before releasing the latch.

Brody took a step back and pushed his hands deep into his pockets. Callie's lemon and citrus scent wrapped around him and tore away the years until they were teenagers again, standing in this barn, as Callie told him she had to leave.

"I'm going to muck stalls." He had to get away. Away from the memories barking at his heels and begging for attention. But before he could enjoy the rigors of physical labor, he needed to remove the horse from the stall. Grabbing a lead rope from the pegs lining the wall, he stomped to the nearest stall and clipped the lead onto the gelding's halter.

Callie held out her hand. "I'll take him out. You want him in the round pen?"

His throat went desert dry as her hand brushed his shoulder. Her fingers wiggled, and he forced his own to relinquish the rope. "Yeah. Round pen is fine. I only use the corral for riding." While he unlatched the door and swung it open, Callie looked the gelding over. "Former track pony. Got too old and the owners sold him. I thought I'd turn him into a kids' trail horse," Brody explained.

Callie nodded. "Seems to have the temperament for it." The gelding leaned into Callie's touch and followed her from the stall with barely a click of her tongue.

Brody snatched the manure fork from the wall and rolled the wheelbarrow over. Leaving it in the aisle, he stepped into the stall. Once he cleaned, he'd get to work on the Appaloosa mare. She was the priority. A quick turnaround and cash flow. He clenched his teeth at the thought. The horses were more than money, but Dad's surgery loomed and the cost would put the ranch in serious debt.

Without a proper and steady income, they might lose it all.

"Can I help?"

He should have expected the question, but it flew in from left field and he scrambled to find an answer. Silence seemed the best response. Sweat trickled down his back as he lifted each load and tossed it into the wheelbarrow beside Callie.

Callie crossed her arms and tapped her toes. "I'm staying with Tenley and your mom invited me to dinner tonight."

He missed the wheelbarrow. The pile of manure landed inches from Callie's toes.

Ice seared his veins and clenched around his heart. Please, no. He'd known he had to work with Callie, but to have her here, every minute of the day...

He took a step back and his heel caught on a wad of straw. One minute he was standing and the next he splatted into a pile of manure. The scent enveloped him and his nose curled. Great. Absolutely fantastic.

Callie draped her arms over the open door and grinned at him. "Looks like you need more help than I anticipated." She started to move into the stall.

Brody held up a hand. Muck slid down his palm. Callie retreated while clapping both hands over her mouth. Laughter slipped out, her joy filling the barn. Horses snorted and hooves stomped. Glow whinnied and pawed the ground.

Brody waved for her to come closer. "Come on, then. Help me up."

Still laughing, Callie grabbed the manure fork and shoved the handle toward him. "Grab hold."

Keeping his grin in check, Brody complied and gripped the wooden handle. Callie braced her feet and gave him a nod. Brody let loose a broad smile and jerked. She squealed and threw out her hands to break her fall, landing with an *oomph*.

She shoved hair from her face. "Should have expected that."

"Yep." He chuckled and wiped his hands over his jeans. They were already filthy, so what did a little more matter?

Callie pushed herself away from his boots and sat back on her haunches while Brody rolled to his feet. It felt good to release a smidgen of the tension riding his shoulders. Callie had always been able to do that, to take his seriousness and help him overcome it with laughter.

"Should I skip dinner with your family?"

His laughter rushed out on a harsh scrape. "Are you

kidding? You're back under the Jacobses' roof. You'll do as Mom says or she'll hunt you down and drag you into the kitchen."

A smile pulled at his cheeks as memories rushed in. Memories of Callie being shepherded into the kitchen for dinner as a teenager when her parents were out of town for the rodeo—which was always.

Callie cracked a smile and stood, bumping his elbow with hers on her way up. "Let's get to work then. If I'm going to earn my dinner, I should muck out at least half these stalls."

"You don't have to do that." He'd been taking care of the barn for over ten years. He had everything under control. Brody gripped the manure fork in both hands and crossed it over his stomach like a shield.

The girl he'd once loved shook her head, sending her ponytail flying over her shoulder. "I'm here and I'm helping. You can't stop me."

Truer words had never been spoken. If he could stop her, she'd have never left him.

An ache spread from his heart. He swallowed the bitter taste of regret. If Dad hadn't suffered the accident, Brody would have been clear to follow Callie. He'd be a big shot by now, with his name in electric lights and people from around the world knocking on his barn door begging him to train their horses.

He'd never understand the why behind any of it.

Lost to his thoughts, Brody could only stand by and watch as she wheeled away and gathered up her own arsenal of stall-cleaning materials. "Looks like that roan mare's stall needs cleaning. I'll take care of it." No questions. No hesitations. She acted as though her absence these last ten years didn't stretch between them like a gaping chasm. No way over. No way through.

As long as she stayed on her side of the barn—and out of his heart—he'd pretend that none of this bothered him.

Six weeks. He could keep from falling back in love with Callie for six weeks. Then she'd be on the road, and he'd be free to return to…whatever this life was that he'd eked out for himself. Without Callie.

Chapter Three

At exactly 6:00 p.m., Callie brushed her clammy hands down her skirt, making certain the billowy material behaved. Tenley ran her arm through Callie's and squeezed. "Relax. Mom and Dad didn't learn to bite while you were gone. If anything, they're more relaxed than you remember."

Was she nervous? Callie's stomach dipped and whirled faster than a roller coaster.

Tenley pulled open the squeaky screen door and pushed Callie ahead. "We're here. Callie's more anxious than a kid waiting for Christmas."

"Thanks a lot," Callie muttered in Tenley's ear.

The younger woman smiled and lifted a shoulder. "Calling it like I see it. They'll smother you with goodwill and maybe not ask a million questions about where you've been and what you've been up to all these years." Tenley's laugh held a tinge of sadness. "Not that they haven't watched you. You're basically a legend around here."

Another shrug and Tenley wandered toward the kitchen as Margaret and Peter descended on Callie with open arms and assurances that there was nothing to be afraid of in their home.

Callie begged to differ, but now didn't seem like the proper time. There was always something to fear. Right now, she and Glow were just one accident away from never competing again.

Margaret patted Callie's cheeks after a fierce embrace and gave a wobbly smile. "You're just in time."

Why did it feel like the woman had a different meaning than being on time for dinner? Callie's palms grew damp again and her shirt stuck to her back as a bead of sweat trickled down her spine. Air blasted from the air conditioner but did nothing to cool the rising heat flooding her cheeks. She'd come back for Glow. Nothing else.

"We'll eat when Molly arrives." Margaret waved for Tenley to join her and the pair headed to the kitchen.

Brody sauntered in, his steps even and without a trace of the worry that had her prancing across the living room to stand in front of the fireplace where photographs lined the mantel. She recognized them from their youth. A picture of Brody the first time he'd sat on a horse alone.

An image of Tenley in her cap and gown at graduation, deep shadows ringing her eyes.

Brody marched toward the kitchen, where he greeted his mother and sister before his voice drifted too low for Callie to hear.

Callie's nails bit into her palms. She caught her breath and pressed her lips together at the photo of Brody and her riding side by side on Glow and Brody's horse Mischief. They were a contrast of light and dark. Glow's golden coat offset by Mischief's black hide. Brody had named him after the colt managed to escape every paddock and enclosure on the property by the time he'd turned a year old.

What had happened to the gelding? Callie replayed the time spent in the barn. Mischief hadn't been in any of the stalls.

"Callie?" The tone of Peter's voice told Callie that he'd called for her more than once but she'd been too lost in the past to hear.

"Sorry." She turned and laced her fingers together behind her back to still their trembling. *Focus on the goal.* Coming back here was the first barrel of the race. They needed a perfect execution of the turn to point them at the second barrel: training Glow to run blind.

They'd conquer the third barrel after that. Winning the championship.

"Something wrong?" Peter gripped the wheels of his chair and rolled backward. He then spun the chair so they were facing the kitchen where the rest of the family gathered around the kitchen table. How many days had she sat there doing homework alongside Brody, Tenley and Molly? More than in her own home since her parents had spent most of her childhood chasing the rodeo.

Callie shook the thoughts away. "What happened to Mischief?" She jabbed her chin toward the picture.

Peter's eyebrows lowered and he frowned hard enough that the former laugh lines turned into trenches that dragged the curve of his mouth down. "Brody sold him."

"What? Why?" Callie's limbs went weak. Brody had loved that horse. He'd spent years teaching Mischief every trick imaginable.

"I'm not certain how much you know about what happened to me, but you should know that I never wanted to hold any of my children back from their futures."

What did that mean?

"Brody's loyalty is one of his best qualities. It's also the one that causes him the most pain. He sold Mischief to pay my hospital bills. What he could, anyway." Peter rolled away, ending the conversation and leaving Callie bereft in a sea of questions.

Molly burst through the door with Luke at her side and a plate held aloft. "Sorry we're late. I brought dessert."

Luke galloped around the room on a stick horse and careened to a stop in front of Callie. "Who're you?"

Callie looked to Molly, but she shrugged and smiled. Callie smoothed her skirt and settled onto her knees, bringing her eye to eye with the boy. "I'm Callie." She pointed at the stick horse. "That's quite a nice animal you have there."

Luke scoffed and gripped the leather that ran around the stuffed head in a makeshift bridle. "It isn't real." He swiped a hand under his nose and eyed Callie. "Uncle Brody promised to give me a real pony for my birthday."

"I said we'd try." Brody swooped the boy into his arms and spun him around, drawing out giggles from Luke. "You deserve the perfect pony, and I'm still looking." He removed his Stetson and lowered it onto Luke's head.

"But my birthday's almost here." Luke dropped his stick horse and it clattered on the peeling laminate. His lower lip stuck out in an adorable pout. "You'll find one, won't you?"

"Luke put in his order for a pony like a customer ordering a custom-made birthday cake." Molly shook her head as she stooped to pick up the discarded toy. She looked from Callie to Luke and back. "Brody has his work cut out for him."

"What has he asked for?" Curiosity pinched at Callie. How long since she'd concerned herself with what anyone else needed or wanted? Living for the barrels had been part of her life for so long that the competition burned within her as a living flame.

And when the barrels fell, she couldn't rely on anyone to help. If Sam knew about Glow, Callie would be forced into an impossible decision.

Molly edged toward the kitchen while motioning for Callie to join her. "He wants a black-and-white paint. But it's more than that. He wants a gelding, something calm that he can ride by himself. Luke has it in his head that, with the right horse, I'll let him adventure out on the trails alone. Reminds me of his father."

Callie waited for more but Molly's lips tightened and the bright sheen of tears covered her eyes.

They stepped into the kitchen together and Callie staggered to a halt. Familiarity filled the room, from the old brown stove to the dents in the wall where Brody had practiced his lassoing as a teenager by throwing the rope at his mom's hanging plants and ended up knocking them into the drywall. Why had no one fixed the cracks?

Margaret helped Peter to his place at the head of the table then moved to his left and sat. Brody took the chair on his father's right, while Tenley and Molly filled in every chair until only one remained…beside Brody.

Callie put a hand to her throat to cover her rapid pulse. No need to let them see how much the simple arrangement affected her. All this time and her place remained. Her chair. Tears pricked and she widened her eyes to stop them from falling.

Brody cleared his throat. "Is this okay?"

No. None of this was okay. Callie longed to say the words beating at her ribs, but she forced them down and nodded while dropping into her seat. It felt like being welcomed home.

"So, Molly, when's the bakery opening?" Tenley snapped the tension, drawing focus away from Callie and giving her a chance to adjust.

Molly threaded her fingers through her hair and leaned away from the table. "Oh, no time soon. I'm still writing up my business plan."

"Let's pray," Peter interrupted as Tenley opened her mouth. The look in her eyes said she wanted to argue, and Callie blessed Peter for jumping in before the Jacobs siblings launched into a heated debate.

They all folded their hands atop the table while Peter poured out a short but meaningful prayer over the food and requested the safety of his family in their endeavors. At his amen, Callie's eyes popped open, giving her a split second to see the family without interference.

Peter winced while moving his hands toward his lap. Margaret dabbed at her eyes with a napkin. Molly and Tenley eyed each other, both grinning like Cheshire cats, and Brody's jaw looked hard enough to crack cement.

Luke tapped Molly's shoulder. "What's that green stuff?"

"Those are peas, Luke." Tenley took the spoon and poured a healthy heap onto Luke's plate. "They make you strong."

"Strong as Uncle Brody?" Luke shoved a bite into his mouth and scrunched up his face as the flavor hit.

Brody piled two scoops onto his plate and winked at Luke. "They taste a little strange, but they make you a better cowboy."

Luke's eyes widened. He gulped down the first bite and reached for another.

She enjoyed watching Brody interact with his family like this. His easy demeanor and natural friendliness focused on Luke, and she caught a glimpse of what Brody would be like as a father. An unfamiliar pang threaded past her defenses.

If she'd stayed, she and Brody might have had a boy like Luke by now.

Brody had given up his dream to stay here and watch over his family when Callie had all but begged him to choose her instead. Her selfishness had known no bounds back then. She'd been angry when Brody had refused to leave, but she'd thought he would follow her. Maybe not right away. But how long could it take to settle the debts of Peter's accident and leave town?

Callie took a closer look at Peter and saw the same face she'd grown up with. Older, of course, with gray threading through the dark brown hair at his temples and in his beard. That was new. Ten years ago, Peter had kept a clean-shaven jaw day in and day out. The rest of his face was the same. A face more familiar in everyday context than her own father's. Deep lines fanned out from cerulean eyes. Worry lingered in the way he watched his family with sorrow bleeding out across his expression.

Peter gripped the wheelchair. His shoulders bore the weight of his family, all while remaining straight and sure. Losing the use of his legs had likely devastated him, but he still smiled and laughed. If a tightness pulled his lips into a frown, he never let it linger but focused on his wife and children. He was a kind and gracious man who never quit.

* * *

Conversation around the table ebbed and flowed like a mare's mood swings. Brody relaxed into his chair and let the words twist around him.

Callie joined in after eating a meager portion of baked chicken and carrots, but she spent most of her time picking at the food while watching his family. What did she see that he might miss?

Brody pushed back from the table and ran a hand across his stomach. "Great dinner, Mom."

"Yes, thank you, Margaret." Callie stood and stacked her dishes. Moving with the familiarity etched into her bones, she brushed the uneaten food into the bowl for the dogs and lowered her dishes to the sink.

When she started to run hot water into the cup, Mom stood and nudged her away. "Don't worry about that tonight. We'll let you off the hook this once."

"Well that's just plain rude." Tenley folded her arms and pretended to scowl. His sister had a terrible poker face, and the edges of her smile pulled free. "I was looking forward to having someone else on dish duty with me. One less day I have to wash."

"Right. Like you do any of the work anyway." Molly scoffed and stacked hers and Luke's plates together. She waved a hand at Tenley. "You end up leaving halfway through the washing and I never see you again."

"Do you two ever stop fighting?" Brody asked the question while watching Callie's reactions play out.

"Only when I feel the need to bicker with you." Tenley chuckled and gathered up an armful of dishes. She moved to the counter and began spooning food from Mom's special dinnerware to the plastic containers that she'd used for as long as Brody could remember.

"Sounds about right. Since it's not my turn, I think I'll head to the house." Brody stood and stretched the stiffness from his back. Shoveling out the stalls had tightened all his muscles into one big knot.

Callie attempted to edge Tenley away from the sink with her hip. "I want to help."

"Then you're on sink duty tomorrow," Tenley crowed, her voice holding an edge of delight. "It's meatloaf night. That means you'll get to scrub out Mom's icky meatloaf pan."

"Tenley," Mom admonished with a flick of the towel toward her daughter. "Be nice."

"I'm always nice."

"Right." Molly rolled her eyes, an action that Luke mimicked. "You're about as nice as a cactus."

"I resent that." Tenley swatted her hand through the water. The splash caught Molly in the face and left her spluttering.

"On that note, I'm out of here." Brody raised his hands amid the bickering.

Tenley spun to face him. "Wait." She twisted a towel in her hands. "Before you go, I have an announcement to make."

The room stilled. Dinner turned sour in Brody's gut. He disliked surprise announcements about as much as his sister loved making them.

Water dripped from the faucet.

Brody waited, body poised to escape.

"I've set up a fundraiser for Dad. Dinner and an auction." She glanced at Callie. "And a rodeo, if I can get enough support."

"Oh, Tenley. You don't have to do that." Mom hugged Tenley.

Dad rolled his chair over and patted Tenley's arm.

What just happened? Did they think Brody couldn't earn the money? "We don't need a handout." His voice came out cold.

Callie's head snapped in his direction.

Tenley gave him a glare that sparked fire in her eyes. "You're the only one who considers this a handout. The town has been trying to put together a medical expenses fundraiser for over a year, and you keep telling them no. You need to let us help."

"This isn't help. This is charity."

Tenley balked. Her chin jutted toward him. "This is our town trying to show support. They want to help."

"Tell them we have it under control." He all but demanded his sister take it back.

"You want me to lie to save your pride?" She shook her head. "Not happening, brother. Get over yourself."

It wasn't about him. He was trying to save Dad from the embarrassment of the town fully knowing how far the Jacobses had fallen.

Brody approached Dad and dropped to a knee. "We don't need this. I can get the money."

Dad patted Brody's hand where it rested on his wheelchair. "I want you to help your sister."

What? Brody's head fell forward. The wheel clipped his chin, knocking his teeth together. He relished the sting of physical pain to drown out the rioting emotions. This couldn't be right. His dad would never resort to accepting charity.

Had he lost faith in Brody? Did he no longer trust him to do what needed to be done?

Well. He'd have to prove Dad wrong. He'd prove them all wrong.

Brody rolled his shoulders and squeezed Dad's fore-arm. He forced his voice not to quiver and reveal his anger. "Come down and watch me work that filly in the morning?"

"Sure." Dad nodded but his mind seemed a million miles away.

Brody turned for the living room and bumped into Callie. She squeaked and ducked back, her cheeks flushing a dusty pink. Heat rose along his neck and he reached to rub it away. "Go ahead." Shame flooded his veins that she'd been a witness to their drama.

She bolted past, called out her goodbyes and shot for the door like she thought the run for the barrels waited on the other side.

Brody followed at a slower pace, both so his family wouldn't think he wanted to be alone with Callie and so he didn't give himself any bright ideas like offering to walk her home. Those days were over.

Gravel crunched under his heels as he strode to his truck. Lightning split the sky and thunder cracked a second later. Brody angled his head upward and waited. The hair lifted along his arms as the air went thick and heavy.

Nothing beat a good storm so long as it didn't damage property or hurt people.

Another bolt shot through the heavens, lighting up the yard and highlighting Callie as she ran down the slope toward the barn and Tenley's house on the other side.

The first warm drop splashed on Brody's nose. He hauled himself into the truck and cranked the engine. Firing up the headlights, he spun the vehicle around and pointed it at the barn, giving Callie enough light to see.

Would she make it before the deluge hit? Brody chewed his cheek and threw the truck into gear. He bumped down the driveway, hitting every shallow ditch and hole he'd meant to fix but had never seemed to have the time for. His head bounced against the truck's roof, reminding him he'd left his Stetson behind. He wheeled a hard left off the gravel drive and turned into the dirt track leading to the barn.

Rain splattered on the windshield and forced him to slow while the wipers swished back and forth. They smeared the water around. It came down too fast, sheeting past the glass and turning the world outside into a blur. Brody slowed the truck to a crawl and drove on instinct. Surely, Callie would duck into the barn to wait out the storm. She knew how fast these things came and went, but he couldn't risk it. He wouldn't risk her safety and the worry already eating at him for not knowing.

He rolled his window down and stuck his head out, tenting his eyes with one hand while he drove with the other. "Callie!" The wind tore his voice away.

The barn lights flicked. On. Off. On. His breath released in a rush. She was safe in the barn. Brody pushed the truck to keep going all the way up to the barn doors. He beeped the horn. One long and two short. Seconds later, the doors rolled open.

Brody pulled inside and cut the engine. Rain pounded the roof and swept into the barn. Callie punched the button to close the doors and stood shivering in the middle of the aisle. Curious horses watched them from every stall, eyes bright and ears pricked forward. All but one. Glow stamped her hooves and released a deep whinny that sent a shiver skittering along Brody's backbone.

Callie spun on her booted heel and trotted to the

mare's stall. Brody couldn't hear over the rain and crashing thunder, but he knew the old Callie well enough to remember her way of soothing Glow. They were meant to be together. Halves of a whole. When Callie rode Glow into an arena, it was better than watching anything else in this world.

Soon, she'd leave him to return to that world. Brody shoved his feelings away, where they belonged. He hopped from the truck and moved down the line of horses. He stopped to speak with each one and passed out bits of carrot from his pocket.

"You still carry treats?" Callie's voice carried over the storm.

He retrieved another sliver and held it out to her.

The old Callie appeared before his eyes. The one who'd snatched his carrot sticks and hid them behind bales of hay or under his saddle. She took the carrot between her thumb and forefinger and inspected it, her eyebrows pulled together and her lip between her teeth. "Looks like you nibbled on this one."

He lifted a shoulder and moved on to a sorrel gelding. The horse bobbed his head at Brody and snuffled up the bit of carrot while Brody combed his fingers through the gelding's mane.

"Tell me about Mischief."

The words unspooled something inside Brody. He bit down on the remark bubbling up, ready to be unleashed. What did Callie care, truly? Pushing the bitterness aside, he ran his palm around the whorl of hair in the gelding's forehead and reached back ten years for words he'd never spoken aloud. "When Dad first woke up after the accident, we didn't know about the paralysis. That came later."

Several days later. By then, Callie had taken off and left Brody with a ring and a broken heart. "That first round of hospital bills nearly sank the ranch. We all scrambled. Tenley and Molly finished school and started working to help out. I knew they couldn't keep that up forever, so I found a man willing to pay big money for a horse like Mischief. Some TV show needed a trick horse."

"And you stayed all these years to keep the place going?"

Brody looked up and found Callie watching him from across the aisle. Rain slowed to a steady drizzle that created a backdrop to every heartbeat. Glow nuzzled Callie's shoulder and she reached up to scratch Glow's favorite spot along the mare's jaw.

He nodded and narrowed his eyes. "Dad has another surgery in two weeks. We still owe from last winter when he went down with pneumonia and spent a week in ICU. You wouldn't believe how much that costs."

"I can't imagine." Callie winced. She took a step and her hand lifted, like she might grip his arm.

Brody eased back and scraped his forearm along the wooden wall. Splinters pricked his skin, the small sting chasing away whatever comfort Callie was offering. "You want me to train Glow to run blind. It's going to cost you. I need this place to be self-sustainable, or at least not a financial drain."

"What about your dreams to travel the world and train all the best horses?"

Her curiosity would be the death of him. He never could resist answering her questions. Even now, the need to fill the silence weighed on his shoulders, pressing them forward. "Maybe someday."

The horse behind Brody snorted and stamped a hoof.

"It's stopped raining." Callie cocked her ear toward the roof.

"I'll give you a ride to Tenley's house."

"Maybe we should run up to the house and pick her up. She might appreciate the ride."

Brody's grin lingered as he rubbed his palms together. "Let her walk. This can be payback for last week when she put salt in my coffee."

"You two are still pulling those old tricks?"

He lifted his shoulders. "You expect us to grow out of it because we live across the yard from each other? If anything, it's gotten worse. Tenley loves a good prank." A thought nudged Brody. He judged it from every angle and found it sound. "Do me a favor while you're staying with Tenley. Find out more about this fundraiser."

"What on earth are you talking about?"

"Just… I'm not sure we should have a fundraiser. I don't trust it." Brody did his best not to intrude on his sisters' lives, but it was his job to keep this family from falling into any more trouble. And Tenley loved trouble with a capital *T*.

Callie made a noise not unlike the horses when he gave them an order they didn't understand. "You can trust Tenley to have the family's best interests at heart."

Easy enough in theory. But he was the person everyone relied on. How did he let go and accept Tenley's help?

Chapter Four

Early on Saturday morning, Brody shifted his weight to his left foot and nodded as Luke circled the corral on the back of a white pony he'd named Snowflake. "That's it, Luke. Keep him going round. Ask for a trot."

He focused on his nephew and refused to let his mind turn to dinner the night before. Or of Callie in that pink skirt. No, sir. He wasn't going to think about her.

Luke poked his tongue out between his teeth and tightened his grip on the reins. He nudged the pony's sides with his heels, and it moved from a plodding walk to a bouncy trot that rocked Luke in the saddle. The boy hung on, though he grimaced worse than Molly when a cake came out of the oven overbaked. "Can we run now?" Each word came with the slap of leather as Luke bounced.

Brody bit back a laugh and coughed into his hand. "Go for it. Steady, though. None of that rodeo stuff. Your mom will never let us work together again."

"Aw, Uncle Brody." Luke nudged again and the pony shuffled from the trot to a canter. The gelding moved slow enough that Brody could jog alongside if the need arose, but Luke had a natural gentleness and presence in the saddle, and Snowflake couldn't be persuaded to overreact if Brody tossed a firecracker under his hooves.

In fact, that was why he'd bought the pony in the first place. The handler at the auction had done just that. The lit firecracker had gone off inches from the pony's front hooves and all it did was blink. Brody had bid on the spot and won.

"Your mother's rules are meant to be followed." Even if he didn't agree with them. He'd been riding sheep at the local rodeo at Luke's age, but Molly recoiled at anything beyond Luke and Snowflake either in the corral or on the trail with Brody alongside. He supposed if he'd suffered the loss of a spouse like Molly had, he might be a bit overprotective too. Molly preferred to say she was cautious.

Horse and rider cantered three laps around the pen before Luke dropped his scowl and relaxed into the motions. A smile began, slow at first then spreading until his eyes squished nearly closed. He whipped off his cowboy hat and whooped. "Look, I'm a real cowboy."

"You sure are." Brody tugged his own hat down and let the pair enjoy the morning.

"Looking good, buddy," Molly called out from the rail behind Brody.

Luke slapped his hat back on his head and tipped it down while keeping up his smile.

This kid was going places. Anything he set his mind to, he'd succeed.

"Okay, slow him down." Brody took a step toward the horse, though he knew it was pointless. Snowflake slowed almost before Brody finished speaking. The gelding was old enough and had been trained enough that he responded to voice commands as easily as rider cues.

Luke tugged on the reins, the slightest movement, and Snowflake stopped in his tracks. "Can we go for a trail ride today?"

Brody resisted the groan curling deep inside. He wanted to go, but work beckoned. Luke was too young to understand that his uncle couldn't drop everything and spend the day on the trails. Much as he'd love to. "Monday." He faced Molly and lifted his chin. "Is that okay?"

She pretended to think it over. Sunlight glanced off her blue eyes until she slid a pair of sunglasses on while she drummed her fingers on the split rail. "I don't know. I'd thought about doing something on Monday. Don't you have a ballgame, Luke?"

"No." The boy pushed against his stirrups until he was standing and peered over Snowflake's ears. "Ballgames are done. Coach said so. Please, can we go trail riding?" He worked his fingers up and down the reins and peeked at Brody. "You can come with us."

Big concession from such a small kid. Luke relished few things more than a one-on-one trail ride with Brody. It was to be expected. Brody was the only male figure in Luke's life who could do things like trail rides. Dad made a great role model, and Luke looked up to his grandfather, but he needed Brody. His brow creased.

Would he ever climb out from under the mountain of responsibility that crushed him?

Callie's arrival had given spark to his dreams, and a wildfire raged on the cusp of reality.

Molly's laughter danced through the air. She had a

way of brushing off her emotions for Luke's sake. Brody knew she wanted to go with them, but she'd allow Luke his "just the boys" time.

She caught Brody's gaze and jerked her head, asking him to come closer.

He obliged. "Luke, you can walk Snowflake around to cool him down."

"How are things going with Callie?" Molly's excited tone boded ill for Brody.

He puffed out his cheeks and folded his forearms over the rail. "Things are not *going* with Callie. I'm helping her horse. That's it."

"Mmm-hmm." Molly wiggled her eyebrows and cupped her hands around her mouth. The image reminded him of their youth, back when Molly loved sharing secrets and couldn't hold one longer than a bucket with no bottom held water. "I heard from Tenley that Callie's been pretty uptight about the circuit. Every time Tenley brings it up, Callie changes the subject."

"Maybe she just doesn't want to talk about it. Especially knowing you two will blab the news all over town."

Molly whacked his arm with the back of her hand. "I would not. I'm telling you because I'm worried about her. Callie, not Tenley. She used to be so upbeat all the time. Nothing ever got her down. It isn't like her to keep secrets and close us out."

"It's been a decade, Molls. People change."

"Some things about people change, but usually, who they are at their core…that stays the same." Her voice dipped low and she ran her thumb along a crack in the fence. "Luke can't remember Brandon."

Words refused to rise past the knot clogging Brody's throat. Luke was barely a year old when his dad had died.

"How am I supposed to teach him about his dad when it's all I can do to say his name without crying?"

Brody gripped her hand in his, wrapping her fingers between his palms. "Luke needs to see you grieve. You think he's not going through some serious emotions himself just because he doesn't know what he's missing? If anything, it's worse because he has nothing to remember, no memories to keep him going."

"Is that how you feel about Callie? You'd rather keep the old, tarnished memories even though they hurt you every time you look at her?"

"Yes." He choked on the word. No matter what, those years were important to him. "Loving Callie helped make me the man I am today. Choosing to stay here while she fulfilled her dreams forced me to grow up, sure, but I don't regret a minute of loving her."

"And now she's back. You have a second chance."

Brody dropped Molly's hand and backed away, slicing his hands through the air. "No way. That's out of the question. Help Glow and earn enough to pay Dad's hospital bills. That's why I'm doing this."

"Uncle Brody, can you help me? I can't reach." Luke's whine gave Brody the excuse he needed to turn his back on Molly.

Luke sat atop Snowflake, but he'd dropped the split reins and they trailed along the ground on either side of the horse's front hooves.

Brody gathered up the reins and passed them to his nephew while making a mental note to switch Luke to a single rein.

"Come on, Luke, it's time to go." Molly waved.

Brody helped Luke from the saddle and eyed his watch. Eight on the dot. Ever meticulous, Molly never left the ranch a minute later than eight so she could drop off Luke on her way into town where she worked at the café. The owner gave Molly use of their convection oven whenever she wanted. An easy trade for a woman desiring to open her own bakery. "See you at dinner." He walked Snowflake to the barn without a backward glance.

Molly's words dug in, hooking and clawing at him worse than a cat forced to take medicine. He wanted no part of a second chance with Callie. Right? He ran his hands up the reins and patted Snowflake's jaw. "It's just business."

Snowflake snorted, his breath blowing across Brody's knuckles. "Thanks. That's what I thought."

After removing the pony's tack and rubbing him down, Brody returned the little gelding to his stall and latched the door. His phone trilled from the office. He debated letting the caller leave a message, but then he'd likely forget to listen. The last thing he needed was to miss out on a potential customer.

He snagged the phone from the cradle and puffed out a breathless, "Hello?" at the same time the answering machine clicked on. It took two tries to shut off the machine while the person on the other side attempted to talk over the robotic voice. Maybe Tenley was right and he should toss the landline. Hardly anyone used them anymore, and Brody carried his cell phone everywhere.

"Can you repeat that?" Brody shifted the phone to his left ear and cradled it with his shoulder.

"I'm looking for Brody Jacobs."

"You found him. Can I ask who's calling?"

A short scratch of pen on paper and the voice returned. "This is Daniel Wells. I'm the owner of a stable out in Bluebell. I heard you're looking for a horse."

Horse? "Sir, I'm a trainer. If you have a horse that needs work, then I'm your guy, but I don't take in horses. This isn't a rescue."

"So you're not looking for a paint? Kid-broke and versatile?" The words directly from Brody's post on a local horse auction site jogged his memory.

Brody cringed and cleared his throat. "Oh…you saw my request?"

"Black-and-white paint. About fourteen hands." The man let out a short laugh. "Son, it's like you snuck into my stable and wrote that piece right from the horse's stall."

Relief rushed in, barreling past his defenses, leaving him light-headed. "Is it a gelding?" He removed his hat and knocked it against his thigh. "My nephew put in a very specific birthday request. You say it's kid-broke?"

"Listen, I could talk all day long about this horse, but I'd rather you come out and see him for yourself. My grandkids have ridden him for the last three years. Taught all of them how to ride and you've never seen a horse take better care of his rider than Ranger."

Ranger. *Thank you, Lord.* The horse even had a name that Luke would love.

"When can I see him?"

"You tell me, son. I'm retired. Nothing for me to do but twiddle my thumbs and watch these horses eat all my grass."

Brody leaned his head out of the office and scanned the barn. He'd planned to work a few horses today, and he'd promised Callie they'd work Glow in the afternoon. He had time. "Expect me around three p.m."

"You got it." The man rattled off his address and Brody scribbled it down on the legal pad underneath his list of chores and the supplies he needed from the feed store when he passed through town. Bluebell was a moderate-sized town an hour south. That gave him six hours to work horses and would ensure his time with Callie was cut short.

His stomach pinched. He wanted to help Glow. He *would* help Glow. He exhaled and returned the phone to the cradle. Time to cowboy up and put his feelings aside. Even if he never trusted Callie again. He had that option. Glow didn't.

If Glow didn't trust Callie, they'd never run another set of barrels. The only way they'd trust each other was to work together.

Trust. Why did it always come back to trust?

Brody hadn't trusted anyone since the night the call came in about his dad's accident. What should've been a run-of-the-mill drive through town had turned into a hit-and-run. Ten years and the culprit hadn't been found. Would never be found. If all things happened for the good, then where was the good in this situation?

Callie paced Tenley's living room for what felt like the thousandth time. She'd already washed the breakfast dishes—if two plates and coffee cups even qualified— and scoured Tenley's bookshelves for something to read.

The wall-to-wall shelves offered Callie any escape she could imagine. Sadly, the only one she wanted was the one she couldn't have. To ride Glow and have the mare soft beneath her leg and responsive to the reins, like she used to be.

She ought to drive into town and grab a coffee. Anything to make the hours pass. Brody promised they'd train today. Late afternoon, he'd said. Callie eyed the clock ticking away the time from its place above the sink.

Shoving her feet into her boots, Callie blew hair from her eyes and then tucked it into the braid trailing down her back. She eased the door open and surveyed the yard.

Brody's voice reached her from the round pen, a quiet cadence that she couldn't decipher except to feel the rhythm of it soaking into her bones. He was leading a red roan toward the barn. She wished for a truce between them, a chance to prove she'd changed.

Why did she always feel the need to prove herself? And why did Brody still affect her this way? Time should have dulled the edges, but it seemed absence might truly have made her heart grow fonder for the lanky cowboy with the velvet voice.

Callie trotted across the yard under the baking sun, dirt and grass crunching under her boots, and joined Brody as he walked the roan.

He didn't slow, neither did he order her away. Since the night they'd mucked stalls together, his stance on keeping her at a distance had grown rigid. It was the same now. His back straightened and his fingers curled around the green lead rope trailing from the mare's halter.

"What are you training this one to do?"

"Working out a few problems." Brody's clipped response didn't bode well for their afternoon together.

Callie pressed on. "Like what?"

Brody turned his head away from her and seemed to find relief in looking at the high mountain ranges cutting across the horizon. "She's a trail horse, except she thinks falling leaves are monsters trying to devour her."

Callie put a hand on the mare's warm hide and patted. The muscle twitched under her palm. "Think you can convince her otherwise?"

"Of course."

Well, at least Brody hadn't lost his confidence. A good thing, considering what they faced in training Glow.

"Are you ready for Glow?"

Brody's silence caused her skin to itch. After what felt like forever, he glanced her way. "Not yet. Something I need to do first."

"What?" Callie didn't regret the question, though she could have said it without the bite of sarcasm.

He walked the mare into her stall and latched the door before answering. "Going down to Bluebell to check out a horse."

"For training?"

He shook his head. "For Luke."

Now she understood. "The elusive birthday horse."

He lifted a hand to the back of his neck. "Yep."

Callie resisted the urge to fidget and pushed her fingers into her jeans' pockets. "I'm going with you." She kept her tone cordial but threaded it with the steel she'd learned to infuse when she didn't want to be told no. Considering the man across from her, he'd probably still argue. Before he could, she tilted her head to the side. "Please. I've been knocking my head against the wall all day. I'm bored to tears."

"You could go for a walk. Drive to town. There are a hundred things to do."

She blew a laugh between pinched lips. "This is Tamarack Springs. Until the fair arrives, there's nothing to do here except drive down to Beruth's field and watch the cows. Or try to hijack your dad's tractor." *Like we used to.* Callie left that off and let history speak for her.

Brody cuffed his cheek and dragged a knuckle down his scruffy chin. "Fine."

An hour in the truck with a silent and brooding Brody meant Callie spent the entire time spinning the radio dial to see how many stations she could catch and how long the music lasted before Brody threatened to toss her from the truck.

The engine rattled but chugged on as faithfully as Brody's old hound who had followed him everywhere during his youth. Even to school.

They passed a dozen empty fields before Brody clicked on his blinker and edged down a gravel lane lined by oak trees. Royal Oaks Stable spread out at the end of the drive. Red buildings dotted the surrounding hilltops. White fences stretched from the barns to the road. Horses grazed in each field. Several lifted their heads to watch the truck pass.

Callie rolled her window down and absorbed the ripe atmosphere.

They stopped at the biggest barn, a monstrosity that stretched two stories. Callie slid from the truck and made certain her mouth wasn't hanging open. A man strode out of the building and held out a hand to Brody. "Welcome. Thanks for taking my call."

Brody dipped his chin. "Mr. Wells, this is a friend of mine, Callie Wade."

"The infamous Calamity Jane."

Callie flushed as the man's eyes lit. "Pleasure to meet you, Mr. Wells."

"Oh, now. Call me Daniel." He waved a gnarled hand. "Ready to see him?"

Callie worried her lip while Brody stared across the fields. "How long have you owned Ranger?" Brody turned his attention to Daniel.

"Raised him." The older man walked into the barn and pulled a halter and lead rope from a long row of hooks.

The barn was pristine. Not a speck of hay littered the floor. Even dust motes seemed afraid to flit through the sunlight streaming inside and lighting up the interior through well-placed vents high in the ceiling. On the other end, a covered arena beckoned. Callie started forward as curiosity welled.

Daniel handed the gear to Brody. "Ranger's in the back field. Go straight down the lane, past two paddocks. You'll find him under the oak trees with his friends."

"You want me to catch him?"

Callie caught the surprise in Brody's voice and almost laughed. Daniel knew his business. She appreciated his approach. He obviously knew better than to have the gelding in the arena saddled and ready to go. Red flag number one when checking out a new horse. To find the horse already caught and saddled often meant the owner wanted to pull one over on an inexperienced rider. They'd wear the horse down and make them look calm, then when the buyer took the horse home, they'd find out they'd bought a bucking bronco.

Brody slung the halter over his shoulder and his chin lifted. She recognized the look; challenge accepted.

"I'll come with you."

"Never expected anything less." Brody muttered low enough that she thought he might not have intended for her to hear.

She waited until they were out of Daniel's hearing before she spoke. "Seems like a decent man."

"We'll see." Brody's short reply came as no surprise.

Thick grass bent under their boots. Callie paused to pluck a blade and roll it between her fingers. Even the alleys between paddocks were sown with quality grass seed. The buildings and land appeared well cared for, the horses clean and allowed plenty of space to graze. Daniel took this place and his horses seriously. "When do you think we can try and run some barrels with Glow?"

"You haven't even ridden her yet, Callie." Brody glanced at her, his stare hard enough to send a prickle along her skin. "I can't answer that until I see how she reacts under saddle."

"Which we're doing today." She made it a statement. Time closed in, threatening to choke her if they didn't get a move on. Glow's comfort was a priority, but if they didn't win the next race, Callie could kiss her dreams goodbye.

Horses lifted their heads as Callie and Brody passed, but none came running to the fences. Sorrel coats flashed in the sunlight. Callie shielded her eyes when a striking bay shot across the field, tail streaming behind like a banner.

"There he is." Brody paused at the gate and watched the small herd swish their tails as they rested in the shade. "Let's see how he goes." Unlatching the gate, Brody left the halter visible. "Here, Ranger."

The black-and-white paint lifted his white head. His ears swiveled toward Brody and he nickered.

"That's right. Come on." Brody held out a hand but didn't hide the halter.

Callie recognized his actions. He wanted Luke to have a horse that was easily caught, and if Ranger took off or refused to leave his herd mates, then Brody would know right away to look for a different horse.

The small gelding shuffled toward Brody and nudged the halter before dropping his head and allowing Brody to slip it into place. He walked toward the gate and the gelding followed, not offering a whisper of protest.

"So far, so good." Callie held the gate and closed it behind the pair.

Brody harrumphed, but Callie caught the hint of a smile playing around his lips as he stroked Ranger's neck. "Let's see how the rest goes."

"Want me to ride him?" Her fingers itched. She needed to feel reins between her fingers and hear the creak of saddle leather. She'd been at the ranch four days and had been on Glow once for mere seconds.

Brody dropped the lead rope and took a step back. The gelding stood and never twitched a muscle. "Looks to understand ground tying."

Callie draped her arms over the gelding's back and waited for Brody to look at her. It took longer than she'd expected, and when his gaze locked on hers, she fought the urge to look away.

He shifted, bringing his arm close enough for her to touch if she lifted her hands.

No. She patted the gelding and slid her hands away while her heart thundered. She could not fall for Brody. Not again.

When she left, he'd stay. The same as before. They were forever meant to circle one another but never to enter the other's orbit.

Barking erupted from behind Callie, tiny yips that told of puppies. She turned in time to see four fluffy blobs racing across the field. They tumbled under the fence and gamboled around Callie's feet. One stopped to gnaw on her boot while a second darted between Ranger's hooves.

The gelding lowered his head and a third pup popped tiny paws onto the horse's nose and yipped.

"He seems well trained." Brody actually laughed, the sound as deep and rich as the mountain gorges.

She'd miss that sound when she left again. Afraid to ruin the moment, she kept silent and leaned to play with the pups.

"I was beginning to think you'd gotten lost." Daniel drove up in a golf cart, sending out puffs of dirt under the wheels. "You want to ride him?" He tipped his head toward Brody, his hat brim casting his eyes into shadow.

"Callie will." Brody passed her the lead rope and scooped a puppy into his arms. The tiny thing wriggled and lunged at his face, sending his hat flying to the ground as it licked his cheek and attempted to crawl onto his shoulder. His laughter returned.

Rough fibers grazed her palms, the feeling grounding Callie to place and time. She clucked and the gelding walked behind her.

"Some guard dogs you have here." Brody's rumbling voice shifted away, and Callie put her focus on the horse.

Daniel chuckled. "You want one? I'll toss one in free of charge."

Callie gripped the lead rope until her fingers cramped

and clenched her teeth before the words could betray her. She'd considered adopting a dog for months now. A dog could keep her company in the truck while she traveled. Unlike Glow, who had to ride in the trailer. Callie chewed her lip. "Where do you want me to ride him?"

"Why not take him into the covered arena? Cooler in there, and Brody can get a better look at how he moves without the sun turning us into cacti." Daniel laughed at his joke and motioned for them to follow him back to the barn.

He pushed out of the cart when they arrived, straightened his button-up shirt and tapped his boots on the barn door. "Tack's in that room there. Take what you need."

Callie followed his pointing finger. Across the aisle, a room straight from the rodeo stared back at her. Row upon row of saddles, each with a bridle hanging on the saddle horn. Blankets were draped across racks stacked three deep in a corner. Silver gleamed on the saddles. "What do you do here?"

"Riding school." Daniel rapped his knuckles on a sign and Callie turned to read it.

Wells Riding Academy.

She'd never known Tamarack Springs or any of the surrounding counties to be successful with a riding school. But it seemed Wells had pulled it off.

"Who trains your horses?" Brody asked.

Callie listened for the answer, only half paying attention as she checked the saddles, looking for the perfect one that fit both her and the horse.

"I did."

Did. Brody's low hum caught Callie by surprise. She eyed him while pulling down a saddle and tossing it over her shoulder. She moved through the actions of saddling Ranger, her years of experience ensuring they entered the arena in a matter of minutes.

Brody and Daniel followed her along the aisle and into the circular building attached at the far end of the barn. Callie stopped a gasp before it slipped out. Daniel had an arena big enough to ride barrels in. An urge to lope the perimeter and speed around a trio of barrels gripped her.

She forced her hands to relax and prepared to mount. Ranger stopped moving when she did and waited. His attention focused on her, Callie swung into the saddle.

Brody called out from the rail. "Take him around a couple times. Put him through his gaits and let me see how he works."

She gathered the reins and nudged Ranger with her heels. Brody was trusting her to ride the gelding that may one day belong to Luke. The knowledge spread through her, a delightful surprise. Progress. She'd begun to think he'd never trust her with anything ever again. But this? This was huge.

Brody loved his nephew beyond measure, and he'd do anything to make certain whatever horse Luke rode was safe.

Callie asked for a faster gait and a smile emerged when Ranger responded. His stride grew long and smooth, allowing her to glide across the saddle.

She felt Brody's gaze, not only on Ranger but on her, and she struggled with an urge to pull out her riding skills and perform for him. Later. Once Glow was better, she'd show Brody that she was better off for having left.

When she finished the ride and walked the gelding to the railing where Brody and Daniel watched with forearms crossed, she kept her gaze turned away from Brody's intensity. The man had a smolder that lasted days and a smile that caused her heart to trip. She firmed her resolve and slid from the saddle. "What do you think?"

"Not bad." Brody's terse response seemed out of place with the way his eyes roved the gelding. He swung around and faced Daniel. "How much?"

Daniel named a number low enough that Callie's mouth popped open. No way this guy was for real. He was practically giving the gelding away. Her eyes narrowed. "What's the catch?"

"No catch." Daniel held up his hands. Hands that trembled until he lowered them to his sides. "I'm getting too old to run the place, and none of my kids are interested in taking over. I'm selling out unless I can find a trainer to take over. My main concern is getting these animals good homes."

"Then you should charge more to ensure that happens." Brody's fingers went white where he held the railing.

Callie understood how much he wanted this for Luke. How dire were his circumstances that he didn't leap at the opportunity to buy the horse for half its worth? The weight of her own selfishness staggered her. In the days she'd been here, she'd not bothered to ask about his situation. He'd given scant details that made her think the ranch was struggling, but she'd pushed that aside as inconsequential because it didn't affect her.

Daniel's smile never faltered, but it changed, becoming weathered and careworn around the edges. "When you've lived as I have, you learn that it isn't always about the money."

Brody's lips pinched into a flat line. He pushed his hat back and rubbed his forehead. "I'll let you know. How long can you give me?"

"Two weeks." Daniel thrust out a gnarled hand and Brody shook on the deal.

Callie bit her tongue to keep from offering to help buy the gelding. Brody wouldn't appreciate her interference. Ten years didn't make him less prideful. If anything, he'd gotten worse.

Chapter Five

By the time they made it back to the ranch, Callie was bouncing in her seat.

Brody scrubbed at his cheeks and turned off the engine. "You still feel like riding today?"

"Absolutely." She jumped from the truck and high-tailed it to the barn before he came up with an excuse to keep her from Glow. Enough was enough. They had five weeks to get the mare running again. Four days of lolling around in a stall was four days too many.

"I'll be waiting in the corral." Brody's voice reached her as she flung open Glow's door.

The mare lifted her head from where she'd been dozing and her nostrils quivered in silent greeting. "Hey, girl. Let's go for a ride." Anxiety wormed its way into Callie, making her fingers clumsy on the halter. Would Glow refuse to move as she had last time? Callie stroked her golden neck and talked quietly while walking the mare out of the stall.

She'd put her tack in the tack room the day she'd arrived, and it sat in the same place, a fine layer of hay dust coating the rich mahogany leather. A quick wipe to clean it, and Callie hauled her gear to Glow's side.

The mare lifted a hoof then put it down. Glow used to dance in place when she saw the saddle and knew it was time to work. Now, her skin shivered and her muscles bunched. Callie's throat turned dry. "We can do this, Glow. You and me till the end." She patted the palomino's firm shoulder and picked up the blanket. She took her time, telling Glow each thing before she did it and ensuring the mare didn't tense.

When Glow's head lowered and her ears swiveled to catch Callie's words, she knew they were ready.

The mare followed Callie into the corral, her strides steady.

Brody stood in the same spot as the day they'd arrived, his posture an exact match for a man who couldn't care less.

"We'll show him, Glow." Callie swung into a saddle for the second time in a day and settled her feet in the stirrups.

Glow felt more like a rock than a horse. The grace and fluidity that Callie relied on were missing as the mare locked her legs. Callie sat relaxed in the saddle and let the reins hang loose.

Her phone vibrated in her pocket. Callie ignored it and focused on Glow. The mare remained tense and uncertain, so she leaned forward and ran both palms along Glow's neck. She murmured and patted, letting Glow acclimate.

The call rolled to voice mail and then started ringing again. Sighing, Callie slipped the phone free. The reins fell from nerveless fingers when she recognized the name flashing on the screen. Her sponsor shouldn't be calling. Knowing she couldn't keep ignoring it, Callie winced at Brody and answered. "Hey, Todd."

"Callie. Where are you?"

"I'm with Glow, doing a little rehab to get her ready for the next race." Technically true. Teaching a blind horse to run again was considered rehab.

Voices chattered in the background. Callie listened but caught nothing more than snatches of conversation. Todd grumbled, his voice muffled, telling Callie he must have moved the phone away from his mouth. She waited and ran her fingers through Glow's mane.

Brody shifted his weight and suddenly it was all Callie could do to breathe with him staring at her like he wanted nothing more than to snatch the phone and toss it away. *Sorry*, she mouthed at him.

He frowned. "I thought you were taking this seriously." His tone bordered on surly and the words threatened to knock the air out of her lungs.

How could she make him see how important this was to her? She needed her sponsors. Without them, she never would've made it this far. Not after that debacle in Oregon when she'd sold more than half her ownership of Glow to Sam. After a rough year of not winning, Callie had faced the choice of coming home with nothing or selling what she had. Back then, she'd thought Sam was a friend. She'd been a gullible fool.

"We need you to come in." Todd came back on the phone and a steady tapping sound accompanied each word.

"What? Why? I'm working right now."

A chair squeaked and the previous chatter stilled. Callie realized then that she'd been put on speakerphone and had challenged her sponsors in front of the entire team. She backpedaled before he blew a gasket. "When and where?"

"Kentucky. I'll send you the address. They want you for a saddle ad. Be there by Monday." He ended the call before she could reply. That was likely a good thing considering the words filling her mind.

Monday? Her phone pinged. Callie tapped the address and added it to her maps. An eight-hour drive.

She went back and read Todd's text. Not only did he demand she be there Monday, but before noon and ready for photos. She'd need to drive up today and room overnight.

Callie dropped from the saddle and stood on shaky legs. What if she refused? The wording in her contract roared up. Unless she considered this ad harmful to her image, she had no choice. The downfall of signing with the first sponsors to offer representation was that Callie had agreed to receive help and money from the wrong people. They told her what to do and where to go, never giving her a chance to live her own life.

"I have to go." She looped her arm around Glow's neck and squeezed the mare. "I'll be back." Tears burned and she forced them down while turning to look at Brody.

He stood rigid as an oak and just as immovable.

"My sponsors need me in Kentucky."

"Glow needs you here." He didn't move, but the intensity of his look bridged the empty space that yawned between them.

Her body went cold. Glow needed her here. But what about Brody? Had he ever needed her? Or had it always been about want?

"How do you expect to train if you're not here?"

Callie straightened her shoulders and walked Glow across the corral. Now that she'd left the saddle, the mare relaxed and followed. She passed Brody the reins. "My contract isn't negotiable. I have to go." She'd said those words before. Four words. Four syllables. They'd hurt the first time she'd pulled away, and they hurt even more now. Her heart ached. She had to leave, and he had to stay.

Brody looked at the reins and then at the mare waiting for his help. He longed to race after Callie, but he'd learned years ago that Callie did what she wanted and no amount of begging could make her stay.

He dropped the reins to the ground. "Stand." He'd taught the mare to stand ground tied as a yearling, and even though he doubted she'd attempt to move, he gave her the order.

In his peripheral vision, Callie retreated to her truck. The engine growled as she put it in gear and rolled toward Tenley's house. He listened for phantom steps that told of her running inside for a bag of clothes.

He couldn't do this. He turned his back on the house and set his sights on the things he could change. The horse he knew how to help.

While Callie drove away, Brody returned to the barn for a lunge line. He raked up his tattered emotions and stored them out of the way. He'd help Glow because the mare deserved to live her best life, a life that did not include fear at every step.

Back in the corral, he looped the reins around the saddle horn while leaving them loose enough not to pull on Glow's bit. He placed a hand on the mare's shoulder. "Away." She shifted from his hand and took a cautious step sideways. "Stop." Glow froze and huffed a breath that caused her entire body to shake and then relax. Good. She remembered the lessons he'd taught her as a filly.

Brody snapped the lunge line to her bridle and backed up to the center of the pen. "Let's see what else you remember." The long rope hung loose between them. Glow cocked her left hind hoof, a sign she'd begun to relax.

If only he could relax. Not only did he have Glow to train alone, but he needed to deal with Tenley's fundraiser idea. No one had said anything since the family dinner debacle.

He hoped it would all blow over, but knowing his sister like he did, he understood the unlikeliness of his hope coming to fruition.

Focus on Glow. He'd take care of personal matters later.

"Away." Brody gave the order and Glow swiveled her head at him. One ear rotated to catch his voice. He wiggled the rope. "Away, Glow." Since the mare couldn't see his body language, he focused his gaze on her and used words they'd practiced years ago.

Glow took a step away from his voice and toward the fence.

"Stop."

Glow obeyed.

Brody settled his weight on his heels and scanned the corral. If Glow banged into the fence, she'd lose all trust in him. She already didn't trust Callie. Not in the saddle, though she followed willingly enough when her owner had boots on the ground.

What had happened on that last ride? He needed to find out. Callie had mentioned that Glow had gone down. He'd assumed the mare had stumbled because of her blindness and sprained the tendon in her leg. But what if it was more?

Walking back to Glow, he ran his hands down the mare's legs, checking for heat or swelling. Callie had said the vet had given Glow the all clear to start practicing again, but he'd not put the horse in danger. Not when Callie proved she was still willing to walk away. From him, and now from Glow, without saying goodbye.

Glow's legs were sturdy. No heat or swelling. Satisfied, he returned to the center of the pen.

He double-checked his position and gathered up a foot of rope, putting a millimeter of pressure on Glow's bit. "Walk."

Again, the palomino hesitated before obeying. One step turned into two, then a full circle around Brody. He let the mare set the pace, let her adjust and take her time. Once she made two full circles, her strides loosened and her body relaxed into the rhythm. Glow knew now that he'd protect her.

He returned Glow to her stall and set out to finish his chores before heading to the house for dinner.

Brody stepped onto Molly's front porch at 8:00 a.m. sharp on Monday morning. The smell of cinnamon slipped into the air. No doubt Molly was baking.

Luke threw open the door and shot out while Molly remained in the living room, holding a boot in one hand and a dishrag in the other. She smiled a worn-out grin and handed Brody the boot. "He'll need that."

"Why don't you go back to sleep? I'll keep Luke busy until noon, give you time to rest."

Molly flicked the towel at him. "No time to rest, big

brother. Do you know how rare it is to have quiet time as a single mom? I'm going to scrub this place from roof to floorboards while blasting music loud enough for Tenley to hear."

"Tenley won't be hearing a thing." The sister in question popped around the side of the house. "I'll be gone all day, so play whatever music you like."

"I planned on it." Molly frowned and crossed her arms. "Where are you going this early on a Monday?"

Tenley fidgeted, twisting her shirt around a finger. "Business in Bridgeport." She turned her back and jogged toward her clunker Toyota. Tossing a wave over her shoulder, she shouted, "See you at dinner. Tell Callie she owes me for washing the meatloaf pan while she was gone."

Callie's name slammed into Brody. He missed her. How could it hurt this much to lose her after less than a week? He squeezed the back of his neck and cleared his throat. He'd spent most of the night scouring the internet for footage of Glow and Callie's last run. What he saw gave him a better understanding of why Glow resisted her rider.

He should have started out with groundwork. If he'd known then what he did now, he'd never have asked Callie to even attempt to sit on the mare until he'd reestablished Glow's confidence. And Callie's.

Luke hopped on the porch on his one booted foot and tugged his other boot from Brody's hand. "Ready?"

Such a simple question. He nodded at his nephew and nudged Molly's arm. "We should talk later."

Her eyes widened.

Luke blasted off the porch and raced for the barn. He knew to wait for Brody at the doors. Even so, Brody turned and watched to ensure the enthusiastic boy didn't attempt anything dangerous. He spoke to Molly over his shoulder. "I may have found a horse."

A sigh spoke leagues to Molly's worries. "Price?"

"Doable." He rattled off the number.

"I'll have to put off the bakery for a few more months."

"You're not required to give Luke that horse, Molls. He's four. He can have the pony he's been riding."

As soon as the words left his mouth, he knew they were wrong. He felt Molly withdraw.

Her voice took on a sharp edge as she replied, "I'll do as I see fit for my son. You're not responsible for us."

Yes, he was. As the oldest, it was his responsibility to keep them safe and cared for, and to make sure that no one needed for anything. If he had to do without, so be it, but not his family.

They'd received another statement from the hospital in yesterday's mail. The monthly payments had been manageable, but with the upcoming surgery looming like storm clouds, Brody prepared to tighten his belt and hold on while the storm raged.

Tenley's fidgeting earlier reminded him about the fundraiser.

"Did you know about the fundraiser?"

"Yes."

"Why didn't you stop her? Or tell me so I could stop her?" He still could. He would. They didn't need outside help.

"Stop fretting." Molly popped him in the back with the towel, the sound snapping Brody from his daze. She put a hand on his shoulder and pushed him toward Luke. "We'll figure it out. I've been saving, and so has Tenley.

We'll help you pay the hospital bills. And the fundraiser is a great idea. You'll see."

"Mom told you." He should have known she'd not keep his involvement a secret.

Molly groaned. "You're a real piece of work sometimes. You know that?"

"I've been told." The steps shuddered as Brody picked his way to the barn while keeping Luke in sight. The boy bounced from the barn doors to the wooden fence and back again but followed all the rules Brody had established.

He saddled up his horse and helped Luke with the pony. "I need a favor, kiddo."

Luke pushed out his bottom lip. "I'm not a kid anymore, Uncle Brody. Miss Lenore says I'm the man of the house." He poked a thumb at himself. Seconds later, his posture deflated and his shoulders curled. "What does that mean?"

"It means that you and your mom are a team. You help her out, right? Keeping your room clean and helping with the dishes?"

Luke toed the dirt. "Sometimes."

Brody refused to put the weight of the title on such small shoulders. He'd carried it since he'd graduated high school, and even he struggled. Luke had every right to be a kid. "Well, my favor includes the horses. I need help with Glow."

"Callie's horse?" Luke perked up. He'd admired the mare since the day Callie had walked her into the barn.

"That's the one. I wanted to pony her while we ride today. That okay with you?"

Luke nodded so hard his teeth clicked. "Sure. Can I ride her?"

"Not yet." Brody led the horses from the barn and looped their reins over the hitching rail. "Glow's blind. She's scared and doesn't know how to live in a world that she can't see. So, we're going to help her learn how to understand what she hears and feels. We'll tie her to my horse's saddle, and she'll be close enough that she can feel his movements when he walks. Then she'll know what to expect."

"You're really smart. I want to be just like you when I grow up. Can you teach me how to train horses?" Luke's enthusiasm lifted his voice and he bounced on his toes.

"Ask me again in a couple months." Brody ruffled the boy's brown hair. "Stay here while I get Glow and we'll hit the trail."

"Can I sit on Snowflake while I wait?" Luke reached for the stirrup when Brody nodded. Together, they fitted his boot into the stirrup and Luke swung into the saddle. He leaned forward and draped his arms on either side of the pony's neck. "I love you, Snowflake. You won't be jealous when I get my horse, will you?"

Brody turned before he gave away the surprise. Luke had the eyes of an eagle and could sniff out a surprise faster than a bloodhound. One look at Brody and he'd be demanding to know when his horse was arriving.

Once he had a lead on Glow's halter and the mare tied to his saddle, he nudged the gelding toward the line of dark oaks bracketing the pastures. They eased into the shade, the horses' hooves thumping on packed earth as they meandered down the trail. He'd chosen this one with Glow in mind. The path ran straight for almost a mile and the terrain was stable while remaining level.

Luke usually tired after an hour or so, and they'd head back. That gave Brody enough time to see how

Glow reacted to unfamiliar surroundings. Callie had been on the circuit so long, he didn't know if Glow even remembered their trail riding days.

The mare rested her nose along his gelding's flank and kept pace. When his horse slowed, Glow did the same. She never tried to move ahead or pull away. If Brody read her right, the palomino was enjoying herself.

Confidence and trust. Two things the mare lacked, but both could be restored. In time.

Chapter Six

Callie yawned and pulled into Brody's drive at sunset on Tuesday. She steered one-handed, the other cradling a sugary drink. Light faded across the yard, casting the barn into shadow and stretching the trees into stark lines that all but begged to be hopped over. She shook her head. The hours alone were wearing her down. Eight hours both ways, combined with a six-hour photo shoot where she'd been angled, positioned and repositioned until she'd felt more like a doll than a person.

The photo shoot had gone exactly as she hoped, and though she regretted every minute away from Glow—and Brody—she was relieved to have the income.

She needed the money from one last win to have enough to pay Sam's asking price without revealing Glow's handicap.

One wrong word and Todd would pull Glow from the circuit. They'd made it this far. One more race. With a blind horse.

Was she risking too much? Glow had given Callie ten great years. She'd never faltered in the arena. Not until that last run when her vision had failed and they'd crashed headlong into a barrel while making a turn. But what a way to go out. Winning the championship on a blind horse would make her unforgettable. Her parents would be proud then. They'd have to be. Callie would have proved that not only was she as good as them, but she'd done something better. She'd earned her place in their precious rodeo.

Callie put the truck in Park and slid out.

Tenley pulled in beside Callie's truck and waved while climbing from the driver's seat. "Well, well, if the prodigal daughter doesn't return." Tenley's smile told Callie the words were harmless, yet they hit something deep inside and resonated. Tenley continued, not noticing Callie's reaction. "Told Brody you were in trouble for scooting out on meatloaf night."

"Sorry. Sponsors call and I go."

Tenley spun her keys around her finger, the clanking filling the air. "Is it that bad?"

"Bad enough that I can't say no." Callie tugged her ponytail holder, freeing her hair and fluffing it with her fingers.

"Can you get out of the contract?"

"Not without a good lawyer or unless they decide to drop me."

Tenley winced. "Ouch. Talk about a rock and a hard place."

"Right?" Callie let out a breath, grateful to have someone understand. "How are things going with the fundraiser?"

"Can I ask for a favor?"

Tenley's question sparked a memory of Brody. He'd wanted Callie to keep an eye on Tenley and the fundraiser. The man seemed suspicious of everyone. She wouldn't be surprised if he asked the grass why it grew in the middle of the driveway.

Callie twisted her spine to work out the kinks from hours of driving. "You sure I'm the right person to ask?"

"You're leaving in a few weeks. Thought I'd better ask while I can."

Point taken. She was leaving. Soon. Why didn't she feel excited about that? The thought of driving off again had her feet feeling heavier than the barrels she raced around.

She held up a warning finger. "Just so you know, Brody asked me to keep an eye on you, so if your favor is something that's going to pit us against each other, I'd rather not know."

Tenley's expression changed from mild regret to pure astonishment. "You're trying to protect him. Now why would you want to do that? I didn't think you had feelings for my big brother anymore."

"I don't. Just letting you know how the score's running."

"I'd say Brody one, Callie none." Tenley pushed open the door. Hinges creaked and complained. Tenley patted the frame. "I know. We're going to get that fixed." She tossed her keys on the counter then jogged down the steps and headed toward the main house.

Curiosity took hold. Callie tried to resist, but she'd been too immersed in this family's life to not want to know. She walked alongside Tenley. "What's the favor?" The looks passing between the siblings often made her wonder if they could read each other's minds. They were so close that Molly had completed Tenley's sentences when they were younger.

Coming back had opened Callie to the possibility of coming home. Permanently.

One more race. Would that be enough to say goodbye to the circuit forever? She was one of the oldest riders on her sponsor's team. Most had hung up their spurs and were happy and settled.

"I want you to help me put the rodeo together."

Callie froze, one foot on the ground and the other on a step. She'd not seen that coming.

"This fundraiser is the out we need. Brody has tried for years to pay down the debt. He refuses to let us help. Except for the times Molly and I have given money to Mom without him knowing. A rodeo would bring the town together."

"I don't know. I'm only here five more weeks. At most."

"The event is in three weeks. Right after Dad's surgery and his expected return home. You have plenty of time."

Callie huffed. "I'll think about it."

"Thank you!" Tenley grabbed Callie into a hug. "This might even help Brody here at the ranch. It couldn't hurt, right? Then I can be here to help Mom and Dad as he recovers."

"What about Brody?"

"Brody's been saying for months he needs another person training horses to keep up with the workload. He's had to turn down three this year from some pretty big clients because he's overworked."

Yet he'd taken on Glow. Callie pinched her forearm to keep from bolting over to Brody's and demanding to know why he'd done that.

Tenley dashed past Callie. "Dad. What are you doing down here?"

Callie looked ahead and found Margaret helping guide Peter along the rocky drive, headed for the corral.

"Brody wanted me to look at that mare. I missed him working her last week, thought I'd give him my expert opinion." He winked at Callie while Tenley stooped to hug her father. "You coming, Callie? Should be a good show."

Didn't she know it. Anything Brody did was bound to set her heart aflutter and make her feel like she was eighteen again. Before she'd left Brody behind to travel the stardust trail of barrel racing fame.

She fell into step beside Margaret. Tenley took her mother's place behind the wheelchair and chattered a mile a minute.

"I'm sorry I missed dinner." Callie directed her apology at Margaret.

Margaret waved a hand. "Don't you worry about that. Brody told us you had to run up to Kentucky for something."

"A photo shoot for a saddle ad."

"Hmm." Margaret's eyes twinkled in the fading light. Crickets started up a chorus from the pond. Croaking frogs joined in, creating a symphony that sounded like home.

"Can I ask something I've no right to ask?"

"What a mouthful." Margaret stopped walking.

Callie did the same and faced the woman she'd once called Mama Margaret. "How serious is it? The surgery, the bills. All of it."

Margaret clutched her shirt collar under her chin and stared across the yard at Peter. "The accident pinched the nerves in Peter's back, causing his paralysis. As the years pass and his vertebrae degenerate, the bones have become weaker. They're concerned that his C-spine, the bones in his neck, will constrict the nerve and cause permanent paralysis from the neck down. Right now, he has what's known as partial paralysis in his lower extremities. He has some feeling, but not enough to function."

"I had no idea." Callie curbed the tears attempting to fall and plucked at her sleeve. "I'm sorry I never called to check on him." She'd not even known about the paralysis until he'd showed up in the wheelchair at the ballgame.

"Did you know that Brody has been offered positions all over the country and he's turned down every single one?"

No, she hadn't known that. Callie's brow furrowed and she opened her mouth to ask how that was related to Peter's surgery.

"Last week, you showed up with Glow, and Brody came alive for the first time since you walked away."

Callie read the implications in Margaret's stiff posture. Brody hadn't been the only one left behind when she'd bolted.

"He mentioned a man in Bluebell needing a trainer, and I know that's only an hour away, but it means that he's dreaming again." Margaret gripped Callie's arms hard enough to tell Callie the woman meant business. "We've prayed that Brody would find hope for the future."

Her heart dropped. Brody deserved hope and happiness. Laughter drifted on the breeze that caught Callie's hair and whipped it onto her cheeks, bringing with it the smell of horses and dirt to tickle her nose.

"What can I do?" Her voice sounded small to her own ears. Across the yard, Brody and Tenley chased each other with lassoes. The red roan mare watched, her body relaxed and ears pricked at the siblings. Peter watched from the rail, leaned forward in his chair like he might attempt to stand at any moment.

It hit her then. What she'd missed all these years. The Jacobses were like family to her, and she'd abandoned them, left them behind as though they had no value to her, and she'd never looked back.

Exactly as her parents had done to her.

God, how did I get to be so selfish? And what could she do about it?

"Help him see that he isn't responsible for carrying the weight of the family. The world may change but God stays the same. You remind him that dreams are worth chasing."

Callie waited, but the matriarch was done speaking. Luke lassoed Brody and the two went tumbling to the ground. Lightning bugs lit up in the field, and Luke barreled between the corral's railings. His whoops drifted on the breeze.

Brody started spinning the rope around his body. Tenley copied him, and they began what appeared to be a competition.

Margaret left Callie standing alone at the edge of the driveway.

Instead of joining the others, Callie retreated to Tenley's house, leaving the laughter behind.

Brody stood on his front porch Wednesday morning sipping coffee as sunlight peeked over the treetops. Summer flared in brilliant greens. After seeing Ranger on Saturday and listening to Luke beg once more for a horse on Sunday, Brody had spent the rest of his afternoon on Monday and Tuesday organizing his schedule in an attempt to find the hours to squeeze in one more horse.

One more job and he had a prayer of staying on top of the bills.

A shadow separated from Tenley's porch and raced for the barn. He lowered his coffee to the porch rail and squinted. He knew that outline. A smile tugged at the sight of Callie sneaking into the barn.

Moving on silent feet, he followed.

Callie's whispers drifted from Glow's stall as soft as feathers. She emerged, leading the mare and continuing her crooning.

Brody put his back to the wall and held his breath. He never should have come down. If he spoke, he'd scare them both.

"Brody?" Callie called, her voice a bare octave above a whisper.

He stiffened. "Here."

"What are you doing?"

"I could ask you the same thing." He pushed away from the wall and moved into a strip of light cutting down the center of the barn. "Going somewhere?"

Callie draped an arm across Glow's withers and gusted out a sigh. "Couldn't sleep. Thought I'd walk Glow around for a while. She's been restless."

"Says the woman who hasn't been here in two days."

"Don't, Brody. I didn't have a choice." She straightened and took a step. "If you're not going to help, then get out of my way."

Sharp words burned the back of his throat and begged to be shot into the void between them. How dare she accuse him when she was the one who couldn't be bothered to stick around to help her own horse? He chewed on the inside of his cheek until the pain edged out his anger. "I was planning on ponying her along on a trail ride today. She seemed to enjoy it when Luke and I took her out."

"You took her on a trail ride? Without me?" Hurt colored her voice and Callie's gaze dropped to the ground. She wound the lead rope around her hand, then unwound it, and repeated the process. "How did she do?"

"Why don't you ride with us and find out for yourself?" No. He'd not meant to offer her the option of coming along. The last thing he needed today was more of Callie's company. She already occupied too many of his thoughts. Even yesterday, while he'd typed up his schedule, his mind had wandered until he'd looked down and found he'd typed Callie's name across half the dates in June. "You can't ride her, of course."

Please let that be enough to push her away.

Callie firmed her stance and lifted her chin. Her cool gaze locked on his. "I'm going to have to ride her at some point, Brody."

"But not yet. Let her find a bit more confidence first."

"When? When can we try again? I'm running out of time."

Brody ran a hand through his hair. Curls fell into his eyes and he shoved them back. "I don't know, Callie. Why not just ride another horse? I'm sure your sponsors have a whole string you could choose from."

Her face went white and she wavered on her feet. "I'm not doing this without Glow."

"Why?" It was the one thing he couldn't understand. "You want to win with Glow, I get that. But why put you both in danger? What are you trying to prove that you're willing to exploit Glow's weakness?"

"I'm not…" Callie shook her head and left the barn. "Forget it. If you don't understand, then there's no way I can explain it to you."

"It's not like Glow cares whether she wins this last run." The words cut the silent morning and sliced between them, severing any potential softening he'd felt when he'd seen her watching him and Tenley.

Callie's shoulders snapped toward her ears and a harsh gasp wrenched deep inside Brody's heart.

An ache settled behind his ribs. Too far. He'd pushed too far. Jogging, he caught up and held out a hand. "I'm sorry. That was uncalled-for." Callie eyed him like she would a snake, making him feel lower than the slippery serpent. "Come trail riding with me. Please. And tomorrow we'll try riding Glow again."

An idea sparked. He withheld it from Callie. Convincing her wouldn't be easy, and she'd no doubt say no if he brought it up now. Once they finished the trail ride, she might be in a better frame of mind to allow the experiment.

"Can I ride the buckskin?"

"Spirit?" Brody knuckled his cheek and peered into the barn like he might see the gelding from there. He lifted a shoulder. "Sure. I'm considering him for the pony rides at the fair this year. You can tell me what you think."

"You trust my opinion on one of your horses?" She put a hand over her heart and exaggerated a gasp. "I'm shocked. Brody Jacobs is letting someone else give an opinion."

"I trust you." When it came to horses.

Callie's look begged to disagree, but she kept her

thoughts captive behind an assessing stare. "Let's go riding."

They were in the woods before the sun fully rose. Brody settled into the gelding's steady stride and wrapped Glow's lead rope around his saddle horn.

Callie rode alongside him, her hat shielding her face from his gaze.

"Will you let me walk her back?" Like before, her voice didn't quite match what he remembered of Callie. She sounded worn. Gone was the carefree girl who'd dreamed big and followed those dreams as far as the road could go.

Brody glanced back to check on Glow, but the mare had planted herself in the same place as before and didn't seem perturbed by her surroundings. Her ears swiveled to catch sounds and though she couldn't see, her eyes moved side to side. He moved next to Callie and Spirit. The buckskin plodded along and never offered any trouble. He'd ponied horses with the gelding before and Spirit accepted it as he did everything. With indifference. "Sure."

"Don't sound so enthusiastic. I might take it personally."

Laughter burst out without his agreeing to release it. The sound burned and forced him to realize he'd not found anything this amusing in years. "Just when I think you've changed, you spout off with something like that and I see the old Callie."

"I'm not the same girl who left."

No. Now she was a woman who'd leave. Time ticked down. Each day breaking his heart in new ways.

"When is your dad's surgery?"

Pain wrenched free of his lungs and squeezed. "Next week."

"Are you going to the hospital?"

He started to shake his head then nodded. "Against everything in me that despises hospitals, yes. I'll be there. We all will be."

"Can I come?"

Brody's legs tightened around the gelding and he slowed his pace until they were hardly moving. He forced the muscles to relax and urged the gelding back to a gentle walk. His pulse hammered. Spending the day in the hospital was one thing. Spending it there with Callie…he couldn't fathom the feelings battering him harder than a ship in a hurricane.

Callie reached up and plucked a leaf from overhead. She spun it between her thumb and forefinger before releasing it to whisk to the ground. "Just because I can't stay doesn't mean I don't still love your family."

His family. Not him. Had his love been so easily removed from her life? Had it not wrenched so deeply into her that removing it felt like dying? Did one look not bring everything all back as though the years hadn't passed, like it did for him? They'd ridden this trail a thousand times over the years, and riding with her now was a certain exquisite torture.

Callie's breath rasped in and out. She shifted in her saddle and inclined her head toward him. "I suppose, if you're opposed to me coming with you, there's no need for me to ask if I can help you train the horses."

"Excuse me? Why would you think I need help?"

"Easy there, cowboy." Callie raised her empty hand. Her mouth twisted to one side, her lips puckering and sending a confusing wash of emotion to compound his tension.

Spirit snorted and sidestepped toward the grass growing along the narrow trail. Callie guided him back and focused on the path. "I'm bored senseless waiting on what little time we're training with Glow. I can help you train the horses. You'd get done quicker and be ready to take on more when I leave. More money for you, and I get to do something other than pace Tenley's living room." She forced out a grin that looked resigned. "I've already counted all her books and organized the kitchen cabinets."

Leave it to Callie to find his weakness. He slid his fingers up the reins and allowed the soft strap to glide across his palms. Leather creaked in time with each hoofbeat. Brody let the sounds fill him until there was no room for anything else. Need overcame precaution. "You remember how to do anything other than run in circles?"

Callie's laughter warmed him better than the hottest coffee. Sunlight caught her braid and dappled Spirit's mane. Even her presence made the day seem brighter. Birds chirped and flitted from tree to tree. Callie patted her gelding's neck and grinned. "I think I remember a thing or two."

"Want to put that to the test?" He dipped his head toward the opening coming up ahead. "Spirit thinks water on the ground is the worst kind of monster. He'd rather jump over a puddle than get a single drop on his hooves."

"Guess you'd better make sure there are no puddles in the show ring when you take him down for pony rides."

"Or you teach him how to walk through them without acting like a fool."

Her expression took on a hardness of challenge that he'd seen every time the camera had found her in the arena. Callie lived for challenges. The more people said it couldn't be done, the more determined she was to prove them wrong. He supposed that was part of why she wanted to keep Glow running.

Callie firmed her jaw. "You and Glow stay there. Let me take him alone." She nudged Spirit ahead, her grip on the reins firm and her seat urging the horse forward.

Brody knew the minute Spirit saw the puddle. His head lifted and his ears went forward. Until then, the gelding had kept his ears toward Callie, listening to her. Now, his nemesis awaited. Callie used her legs to keep pressure on and clucked her tongue. "Walk on, Spirit."

The gelding stepped up to the very edge of the puddle and then bunny hopped over it.

Callie laughed, a full belly laugh that forced Brody to smile. No one could hear that childish sound and not respond in kind. She was enjoying this.

She turned Spirit and walked the gelding back to the puddle. This time, she stopped him one stride away from the water. A puddle no bigger than a birdbath and the gelding acted like the Loch Ness monster might leap up at any moment and swallow him whole.

Callie dropped from the saddle. "Does he like baths?"

"Not particularly. Doesn't fight them, but is more resigned than anything."

She walked around the horse, hands planted on her hips. Her nose scrunched. "What's the deal then? You're not afraid of water, you just don't want to walk through it?" Backing up, Callie put her heels at the edge of the puddle.

Spirit used his nose to bump her and Callie took a step back, into the middle of the brackish water. Golden ears flicked.

Callie lifted a boot and stomped. Mud sprayed across Spirit's fetlocks and splattered his knees. The horse snorted and twisted his head.

Brody crossed his wrists over the saddle horn and watched. Glow nuzzled the saddle then moved close enough to nudge his leg. "What's your girl up to, huh?" Brody spoke to the mare before reaching over to pat her neck. They stood there together while Callie continued her work with Spirit.

Years unwound, putting Brody back in high school when they'd first started training Glow. Where he had a methodical approach and could read a horse's body language, Callie had an innate sense of what horses needed.

He could see her use that now as she took another step back and put both hands in the muck.

Spirit lowered his head to Callie's and knocked her hat aside. Once it was out of the way, he worked his lip across her scalp and then down her arm. When he reached the water, he stopped, raised his head and let out a trumpeting sigh.

Callie stood and elevated her arms, letting the mud drip from her fingertips.

Spirit lifted a hoof, set it down, then lifted it again.

Brody quirked his eyebrows when Callie did the same, only she set her boot down in the middle of the puddle, raised it, then splashed again.

The horse shook his head, sending his mane flying side to side, and shivered all over, rattling the stirrups.

Brody clamped his teeth together before he asked a question and ruined the moment. This was the Callie he remembered.

The one in the arena was fearless and confident, same as the Callie he knew, but this version had a peacefulness that seemed to be missing when she gave interviews and showed up in ads across the Western tack world.

"You mind giving me a hand?" Callie glanced over her shoulder and lifted her palms. "I might have gotten ahead of myself."

Brody swung from the saddle. "Not sure what you think I can do. There's no fresh water around here."

Callie's grin turned devious. "Oh, it's not about getting clean." She grabbed his shirtfront and jerked him into the water.

His boots landed and squelched. He windmilled his arms to stay upright. Spirit stuck out his head, offering Brody the chance to grab his mane. Snatching a fistful, Brody kept his balance and glared at Callie. "What was that for?"

She pointed down.

Spirit stood with both front hooves in the mud. He lowered his head and huffed on Brody's boots then raised a hoof and put it back down in the puddle.

"He just needed a reason."

"Why go into the mud when you can go over it? Well, you were stuck in the middle, so he had no choice."

"You talk about him like he's a person." Brody gripped Spirit's neck and pulled his boots from the mire. They came loose with a slurp.

Callie shrugged a shoulder. "After years on the road with no one to talk to but Glow, I think of them as friends." She walked to the edge of the trail and wiped her hands across a bundle of grass until she'd removed most of the mud.

Brody did the same with his boots on the other side. "So, do I get the job?"

Brody swung into the saddle and gathered his reins. "Sure. If I find another horse that needs to learn how to play in the mud, I'll know who to call."

"Hey." Callie flicked her fingers in his direction, shooting flecks of mud onto his thighs. "I can do more than that."

Didn't he know it. A smile teased its way to the surface.

Callie mounted and glared while tucking her feet into the stirrups.

He handed her Glow's lead and their fingers brushed. Everything in him wanted to reach for her hand and hold it tight. Her inhale told him the effect was mutual. Unwillingly, his gaze found hers and the pools of emotion pulled him down until he thought he'd drown there. These moments reminded him of all he'd lost when she'd left and all he might gain if she ever chose to stay.

He leaned closer.

How many times had they ridden this trail for the peace and solitude it provided? How many hours had they spent under the midnight sky while making promises of forever?

They no longer had a forever.

Brody pulled back and straightened in his saddle. He'd almost kissed her. One trail ride and he was ready to jump back into that life, into Callie's circle.

"There's a gray mare in the stall beside Glow's. She

doesn't like to pick up her hooves for the farrier. You can work with her today and ride Glow tomorrow."

He urged his gelding toward the barn. A need to gallop away twisted, but Brody resisted. Glow wasn't ready, and he didn't want Callie trying to follow him with the mare in tow.

Angry at himself for nearly succumbing to the radiance that Callie shone into the world, he flexed his fingers to keep them from curling into fists and focused on the trail.

Whatever he and Callie once had, it was over.

Chapter Seven

The next morning proved as difficult as he'd expected. Brody put his shoulder to the rail and crossed his arms as he stared at Callie.

She planted her hands on her hips, reins trailing over her forearm. "You can't be serious."

"You've no idea."

"I haven't been led around on a horse since...forever." Her nose scrunched. "Honestly, Brody, if you're out to embarrass me, there are better ways."

"You think I would waste my time trying to embarrass you?" Her accusation cut deeper than he thought possible. He batted the pain away and drummed his fingertips across his shoulder. "Up to you. We do this my way or not at all. You're here to help, but that doesn't mean you get to challenge my methods. If you think you can do this on your own, there's the gate, and it's wide open."

With every word he spoke, Callie's shoulders dropped until her hands fell to her sides and her gaze slid away from his. Shame? Or something else? "Nice attitude. You talk to all your friends that way?" Her jaw worked and her cheeks flushed, and he knew then that she was trying to rein in her temper.

"You're not my friend. Not anymore." He pulled in air through tight lungs and pushed off from the rail. "Sorry. Seems my person-to-person needs a little work. This is why I didn't take a job where I had to deal with people."

"I heard that Daniel offered you a job. Why didn't you take it?"

How had she heard about that? The out-of-the-blue call had come while she'd been in Kentucky. He'd told his parents but no one else.

Right. That explained how she knew.

"I have enough work here. I don't need his charity either."

"What is it with you and perceived handouts? It's a job, Brody. A job you love. Did you not see the quality of horses he had in those paddocks?"

"I saw. Not interested." He patted Glow's neck and then moved to squeeze Callie's arm. The move held a hint of regret, even though he released her after a mere second. "I'm sorry. I'm taking my frustration out on you, and that's not fair."

She exhaled softly and rolled her head from side to side. "You need to stop treating me like an enemy." She quirked one side of her mouth upward. "When it comes to Glow, I'm impossible to get rid of."

"You still stand with her when the farrier visits?"

A shy grin slipped over her face. "Guess you'll find out when he comes to reset her shoes. We'll see if I can get that mare to stand still while he's here." She draped the reins over Glow's withers and prepared to mount.

"My farrier is a woman."

Callie paused, one foot in the stirrup. Her mouth popped open. "Really? Fred retired?"

"Yeah. His daughter took over the business."

"That's great. Good for her. She was always following him around when we were kids." Callie swung into the saddle and gathered up the reins. "Okay. What are we doing?"

Brody chewed his cheek to keep from grinning. If she resented his first idea, then she was bound to despise this one. He pulled a bandana from his pocket and held it up.

"What's this for?"

He pointed at his eyes. "You need to know what it feels like for Glow."

"You want me to ride blindfolded?" Her nose did that thing again, and he battled a rush of affection.

"That's why I'll be leading you." He motioned at the three barrels spaced evenly in a triangle around the pen. He'd measured everything to perfection. The barrels were regulation, everything Callie needed for official barrel racing training.

Callie looked across the arena and chewed on her lip. She took the bandana, and he noted how careful she moved, as though a single touch from him might poison her. "I would ask you to explain, but I get the feeling you're making it up as you go along."

"All good trainers have their tricks." He swiped a hand over his mouth to erase the grin.

Callie took off her hat and sent it sailing toward the rail. Then she folded the red bandana and wrapped it around her eyes, tying it behind her head. She groped for the reins, every movement stiff.

Brody noted the difference. When she could see, her

movements were fluid. Without her sight, she tensed. Putting off the exercise would only compound her discomfort. "Ready?"

"Not at all." She reached for the blindfold.

Brody gripped her leg just above her boot.

Callie twitched away.

Glow pranced in place and snorted.

"Sorry." Callie's wispy apology barely reached his ears. She inched her hands forward until she reached Glow and patted twice before returning her hands to the saddle, where she gripped the saddle horn until her knuckles went white.

"You know how people say that horses can sense fear?" He kept his voice soft and let the question linger.

Callie gave a jerky nod. "What does that have to do with Glow?"

"How fast is your heart beating right now?"

Callie hesitated then released a rush of air. "It's pounding. It's been that way since we crashed. I've never taken a fall that hard before."

The admission had to pain her, but he knew she'd been truthful. Falling was part of riding, but even a professional could feel fear. "Glow can hear your heartbeat from up to four feet away. It's how they've adapted to sense danger. It's how wild horses know when to run away."

She tapped her fingers along the saddle and ran them into Glow's mane. Nothing he said came as a surprise—they'd both learned it years ago—but the reminder seemed to help her relax.

"You need to ask yourself why you're afraid. Why does sitting in the saddle make your heart race with fear?"

"How does she know the difference? When we're heading out for a run, my pulse is fast then too."

Brody patted her calf.

Callie nearly bolted from the saddle.

"That's how she knows. You're tense as strung wire. You stopped trusting her when you two fell."

"And she lost her confidence in me."

Brody squeezed again. "Take a breath." She did as he requested and he released his grip. "We'll take it slow. There's nothing to worry about. I'm here."

Callie's head jerked in a nod. "Let's do this."

He held the reins under Glow's chin and clucked his tongue. "Let's go, girl."

Glow took a hesitant step then another.

Brody murmured the entire time they approached the barrel to the right of the gate. "You still go right, left, left?"

"Yes." She didn't hesitate, knowing right away what his question meant. Right around the first barrel, left around the second, left around the third, then a run home.

When he started to turn right, Callie clamped her knees on Glow's ribs. The mare stopped in her tracks. "I can't do this. How am I supposed to run if I can't see?"

"You're asking Glow to do it." Brody pointed out the fact in a calm tone. He needed Callie to understand the trust Glow had in her rider, and the trust Callie needed to place in Glow. "You two stopped trusting each other."

"It isn't that simple."

He looked back, taking his time. Knowing Callie couldn't see his expression, he let the emotions fall over him. "It is. Trust your horse, Callie." He hesitated, but the words would not be denied. "Trust me. I'm right here. I won't let you fall."

"Do you know why I left?"

He stilled at the change in conversation. His heart drummed. "You were following your dreams."

Her fingers flexed. "Yes. And no." She swallowed, her throat dipping hard. "I left because I didn't have the strength to tell you no again." A tear slipped free of the bandana and trickled down her cheek. "I knew that if you asked me to stay, I would've agreed."

"And you'd still be here, living a life you never wanted."

"I never said I didn't want this life." She wiped at the tear and sniffed. "I just wanted to chase down my dreams first. I always thought I'd end my career and open a riding stable."

"You still want to teach?"

"I never stopped wanting to teach. But the rodeo wouldn't wait."

Brody knew the statistics. How most rodeo careers ended at the age of thirty, bodies too broken to continue. He closed his eyes and released a knot from his shoulders. He understood Callie's drive. She'd followed her dreams while he'd set his aside. If he'd been able to think straight back then, he might've known, but fear and anger had clouded his judgment. He'd wanted Callie here, by his side, for his own comfort.

She took another shuddering breath. "How am I supposed to do this, Brody?"

"Just hold on."

Callie removed the blindfold. He couldn't fathom why she'd kept it on this long. Her gaze met his and her voice shifted to something close to fear. "Not just this. Everything. Going back to the rodeo. Riding a blind horse in a competition. Have I gone too far?"

His chance to convince her to give up the rodeo.

Brody rolled the idea around and found that the thought soured his mind. "I've seen blind horses jumping hurdles five-feet tall. If they can do that, then Glow can learn to run barrels with you as her eyes."

She stared into Brody's eyes until he thought she might leap from the saddle and take off running. After a moment that felt like forever, she pulled the bandana back on. "Let's go. I trust you."

Three words never meant more to him. Of all the times she'd claimed to love him when they were teenagers, he'd never felt closer to Callie than he did right now. The words settled deep and eased the wound she'd created by leaving.

He patted Glow's neck and took up the reins again. "Okay. Let's think this through. When Glow could see, she anticipated the turns. From the minute she saw the barrels, she knew what was coming. We taught her what to expect. How are you going to let Glow know what's coming when she can't see the barrels?"

"Walk us around the barrels. Let me get a feel for her movements. I should be able to do this with my eyes closed…pun intended. I didn't realize how scary this was." She wiggled in the saddle. "When we start a turn, I always grab the saddle horn." Callie mimicked the action, and Glow lifted her nose.

"She knows that, but by the time you reach for the horn, she needs to already be preparing for the turn." Brody took a step back. "Glow responds to the pressure of the rein, so you're putting the rein on her neck, asking for the turn and gripping the saddle horn. What if you tap her neck on the side you want her to turn in to? That will signal her to anticipate your next move.

Glow knows this pattern. After ten years, she can run it blind, she just needs more help."

"How does the blindfold help me in this situation when I can't see the barrels either?" Callie's nervousness had dissipated and she no longer clung to the saddle horn.

Brody let the pair have a moment to settle in as he faced the barrels again. "I'll communicate what's coming, and you share that with Glow."

"So this is like one of those trust exercises some big corporations do to get their teams to work together."

"Something like that." He'd gotten the idea from Daniel after their visit. The man had skills. Brody could beat his head on the nearest barrel for not knowing the man lived a mere hour away. Not that he had time to drive down on a whim just to sit and pick the man's brain over training techniques. Though he'd certainly take his time later when he returned for Ranger.

Molly had given the go-ahead and the gelding's vet check had come back clean. Looked like Luke was getting a horse for his birthday after all.

"Why are we still standing here?"

Brody shook himself free of his train of thought. "We're about two steps from the start of the turn. Glow's strides are short right now because she's still uncertain. That means her walk around the barrels will take a lot longer. When you feel her right shoulder take that second step, pat her neck then start moving your rein. I'll tell you when the turn's almost done."

Callie nodded. Under the bandana, her mouth flattened into a thin line. Glow caught Callie's emotions and, for the first time, a sheen of excitement seemed to gather in the mare's muscles. She took the two steps, and Callie followed his instructions. Brody led them a full turn. "Straight shot to the second barrel. Same procedure, opposite side."

They repeated the procedure two more times, coming around the third barrel at a steady walk. A grin split Callie's face. "See if she'll run."

"Are you sure?"

Callie nodded once and kept the blindfold in place. "We trust you. Take us all the way home."

Home. What a wonderful word. Brody breathed deep and clucked at Glow. "Quick, Glow." As she did in the corral, Glow responded to the words he'd taught her as a foal. Her first step was clumsy as she worked to find her footing. Callie kept her seat relaxed and Brody focused on their path. He jogged beside the mare. "Quick, quick." He clucked and Glow responded, breaking into a shuffling trot. Brody let her find a rhythm where she felt comfortable, and her gait smoothed.

He eased her to a stop a few yards short of the rail. "Well, it wasn't very smooth, but she went faster."

Callie's grin threatened to break through every cloud in the sky and send sunshine pouring on them with the intensity of a meteor. "She did it." Ripping the bandana off, Callie jumped from the saddle and hugged the mare. "Way to go, Glow. I'm so proud of you."

She turned to Brody next and her arms went around his neck. "You're the best, Brody. She's going to do this. One day and she's already responding. In a few weeks, she'll be just like the old Glow."

He didn't know about that, but he couldn't bring himself to burst Callie's hope. He clung to the moment as his arms went around her. "No matter how long it takes, I'll be here to help." He ground every emotion into the promise. No matter what, he would not let Callie down again. She'd given him back a piece of his heart when she'd admitted why she'd left, and he'd cherish that forever.

Callie didn't know why she'd bothered telling Brody the truth. It had come out in the silence and anonymity the blindfold had provided. Watching him help her had drawn lines she'd known better than to cross. Still, their old familiarity lingered and tugged, begging to be reinstated. She returned Glow to her stall and took the mare Brody asked her to train. She skip-stepped where Brody couldn't see and smothered her laughter behind her fist. The mare nudged her palm and obeyed her order to stop.

Brody was letting her train. One of his horses. Well, a horse that someone wanted him to train. She'd done an internet search on him last night and found next to nothing. It spoke well of his training that he had consistent business without a website or any advertising save word of mouth.

She ran her hands down the mare's sides and legs. The mare kept still until Callie touched a hoof. Even then she did little more than shift toward Callie. The gray head swung around and the mare nibbled Callie's hair. She tugged at the fetlock and raised the hoof. Callie held for a count of three then released. The mare wiggled her upper lip.

"Whatcha doin'?" Luke's childish voice rose from Callie's left.

She straightened and blew hair from her eyes. "Training. What about you?"

Molly and Luke watched her from outside the corral. Luke tucked his chin into the rail and sighed. "I'm training too."

"What are you training for?"

"To ride by myself." Luke's tone turned petulant. He eyed Molly, face downturned into a frown. He became the picture of dejection.

Brody swooped in from behind Luke and swept him into a spin. "What's this? You tired of our trail rides?"

Luke giggled. "Never." He sobered and wiggled to be let down. "I'm a big boy. I can go by myself."

"I always thought riding alone was never as much fun as being with someone else." Callie lifted a rear hoof and held it for five seconds.

"Really? But you always ride alone."

Luke's words hit harder than a wrong turn on a barrel.

"He watched you on the internet. Found your runs uploaded on a rodeo site. He's been watching nonstop," Molly explained with a grimace.

Callie's mouth went dry. She'd known people watched her, but to have that fact put in her face here and now, at her home turf, shook her. Everything, every run, was out there for the entire world to see. Her sponsors put her face on products and called her a role model, but that had never mattered before.

Knowing Luke watched her every move, past and present, Callie brushed off her hands and approached Luke. She dropped to a knee. "Those runs you saw, those are only part of it. The other twenty-three hours out of the day, I'm training, practicing, but my friends are there. We cheer each other on." On a good day. On the bad ones... She'd not tell him about those. Rose-colored glasses could be worn a while longer for the four-year-old.

"Do you trail ride?" Luke cocked his head and turned expectant eyes at his mother.

Callie grinned. "Definitely. Not in a long time until I came back here, but trail riding is one of my favorites." She caught Brody's eye and dared to release a tiny smile.

He tucked his hands into his pockets and spun away, whistling.

"Mine too." Luke reached up and took his mother's hand while staring past Callie at the mare. "Will you come to my birthday party? I want to do that." He pointed at the barrels still in the corral.

Callie arched her eyebrows at Molly, who raised a shoulder in a move that said the choice was up to Callie. "Sure. When is your party?"

"Saturday," Molly answered when Luke waited too long.

Saturday. Callie stood and held out her hand to Luke. "I'll teach you to race if you agree to teach me to lasso."

"Okay." Luke bounced on his toes and leaped onto the rail. "Can we start today?"

"After this. Let me finish my work." She pushed up and drifted backward. The gray mare waited for her, perfectly patient. She moved to the far side, cutting off her view of the small family. Her heart pinched.

Luke kicked at the grass and skipped toward the barn.

She continued lifting hooves, holding each for a few seconds and then lowering it to the ground. The mare allowed her to hold the hoof for ten seconds before she started trying to play. The mare never became rude or belligerent.

Callie moved to her head and stared into the brown eyes. Curiosity burned there.

Brody approached from the barn. "Found the problem yet?"

"What does she do with the farrier?"

"Nothing."

Callie spun. Indignation burned her stomach. "What do you mean?"

"She's a tricky one. Does fine at first. But the longer it takes, the more annoyed she gets. One minute she's a lady, the next she's pulling Lily's tools out of the box and tossing them around."

"I think she's bored. Have you tried distracting her when the farrier's here?"

"What do you expect me to do, toss her a ball?"

Callie led the mare to the barn.

Brody opened the gate for her.

"You could." She wound the lead rope around her arm as they walked past Brody. "It's better than having her chuck a rasp at your head. What's her history?"

"I don't know much. Current owners bought her at auction for their daughter. Found out about the hoof issue and brought her here."

"What are they using her for?"

The mare hurried inside the stall and shoved her nose into the hay net. She ripped off a chunk and mouthed it noisily.

Brody stood beside her, their shoulders touching. "Hunter jumper."

"Makes sense then. She's constantly evaluating and assessing. Always in go mode. No wonder she's bored standing still." As though to prove her point, the mare paced across the stall and bopped her head. "You have a Jolly Ball?"

"I think there's one in the tack room. Still in the box." He put his back to the stall and scratched his cheek. "I'm going to pick up Ranger tomorrow night. You want to ride with me?"

"Only if we take my rig." More like her sponsor's than hers.

Brody stuck out his hand. "Deal. But only if I drive."

She slapped her palm to his, ignoring the way his calluses fit perfectly into her hand. "Deal. Pick me up at five."

Brody held her hand a moment too long and her heartbeat shot into overdrive. This touch raced through her, adrenaline shooting faster than when she ran barrels. Callie pulled loose from his hand. "I'm going to tack up Glow."

"You just finished working with her."

"Glow's used to exertion. We're running out of time and I don't want her to lose what little edge she has left." Callie spun away before she did something foolish, like ask Brody to join them. "We can use the exercise."

"Want me to help?"

Her heart skipped. Callie pushed the emotion away and shook her head. "I'm just going to walk her around the barrels. Talk to her."

"Are you going to ride?"

Was she? A lump knotted in her throat. She ignored that, too, and palmed the back of her neck. "We need the practice. If I can't get her to walk around the barrels with me in the saddle and without you leading us, then there's no need in us continuing the training."

"It's been one day, Callie. Cut yourselves some slack."

YOU pick your books –
WE pay for everything.

You get up to FOUR new books and a Mystery Gift...
absolutely FREE!

Total retail value: Over $20!

Dear Reader,

Your opinions are important to us. So if you'll participate in our fast and free "One Minute" Survey, YOU can pick up to four wonderful books that WE pay for when you try the Harlequin Reader Service!

As a leading publisher of women's fiction, we'd love to hear from you. That's why we promise to reward you for completing our survey.

IMPORTANT: Please complete the survey and return it. We'll send your Free Books and a Free Mystery Gift right away. And we pay for shipping and handling too! *We pay for EVERYTHING!*

Try **Love Inspired® Romance Larger-Print** and get 2 books and fall in love with inspirational romances that take you on an uplifting journey of faith, forgiveness and hope.

Try **Love Inspired® Suspense Larger-Print** and get 2 books where courage and optimism unite in stories of faith and love in the face of danger.

Or TRY BOTH!

Thank you again for participating in our "One Minute" Survey. It really takes just a minute (or less) to complete the survey… and your free books and gift will be well worth it!

If you continue with your subscription, you can look forward to curated monthly shipments of brand-new books from your selected series, always at a discount off the cover price! Plus you can cancel any time. So don't miss out, return your One Minute Survey today to get your Free books.

Pam Powers

"One Minute" Survey

GET YOUR FREE BOOKS AND A FREE GIFT!

✓ Complete this Survey   ✓ Return this survey

1 Do you try to find time to read every day?
☐ YES   ☐ NO

2 Do you prefer books which reflect Christian values?
☐ YES   ☐ NO

3 Do you enjoy having books delivered to your home?
☐ YES   ☐ NO

4 Do you share your favorite books with friends?
☐ YES   ☐ NO

YES! I have completed the above "One Minute" Survey. Please send me m
Free Books and a Free Mystery Gift (worth over $20 retail). I understand that I ar
under no obligation to buy anything, as explained on the back of this card.

☐ **Love Inspired® Romance Larger-Print**
122/322 CTI G2AK

☐ **Love Inspired® Suspense Larger-Print**
107/307 CTI G2AK

☐ **BOTH**
122/322 & 107/307
CTI G2AL

FIRST NAME _____ LAST NAME _____

ADDRESS _____

APT.# _____ CITY _____

STATE/PROV. _____ ZIP/POSTAL CODE _____

EMAIL ☐ Please check this box if you would like to receive newsletters and promotional emails from Harlequin Enterprises ULC and its affiliates. You can unsubscribe anytime.

LI/LIS-1123-OM

◆ HARLEQUIN® Reader Service — Here's how it works:

BUSINESS REPLY MAIL
FIRST-CLASS MAIL   PERMIT NO. 717   BUFFALO, NY

POSTAGE WILL BE PAID BY ADDRESSEE

HARLEQUIN READER SERVICE
PO BOX 1341
BUFFALO NY 14240-8571

NO POSTAGE
NECESSARY
IF MAILED
IN THE
UNITED STATES

"There's no time." No time for falling in love with Brody. No time for taking this the slow and easy way. No time for giving up her dreams. "Glow can do this. And so can I." She spoke low enough that Brody couldn't hear, saying the words for herself, needing to hear them out loud. They could do this. She and Glow had been a team far too long to give up now. One more run. One more win and she'd have enough to buy Glow back from Sam.

An hour later, Callie sat atop a barrel while Glow rested her head on Callie's lap. She combed the blond forelock and ran her hands over the palomino's ears. "We can do this." She put her hands under the mare's jaw and lifted her head to stare into Glow's eyes. It didn't matter that she couldn't see. "It doesn't matter." Callie calmed her racing pulse and put her cheek to Glow's forehead.

Glow nibbled on Callie's shirt and snorted.

"Right. Let's do this." Callie dropped to the ground and moved to Glow's side. She tightened the cinch and swung into the saddle.

Glow weaved her head side to side.

Callie sat frozen as fear crept in. Their crash played through her mind. Her breathing went ragged and her grip on the reins tightened. "No. No fear. We can do this." She relaxed her body one muscle at a time and then asked Glow to turn. The mare responded. Her steps were slow, methodical, but she moved. For the first time since she went blind, Glow trusted Callie to guide her from the saddle. Elation swelled, replacing the fear.

They walked to the gate and Callie turned Glow around. "Slow and steady. Just like we practiced." She nudged with her heels and Glow responded, trotting toward the first barrel. Callie gave her notice of the turn, patting Glow's neck before gripping the saddle horn and leaning into the turn. She didn't bother attempting to make a tight turn. Glow wasn't ready for that, and her thundering pulse said neither was she. All she wanted was a clean run. Time ceased to matter.

Glow spun on her hindquarters and lined up for the second barrel. Callie tamped down a whoop and trotted through the pattern they'd completed thousands of times over the years. As they rounded the third barrel, Callie leaned forward. "What about it, Glow? Should we run?" She asked for speed, and Glow answered, pushing off with her hindquarters and sailing down the middle of the corral.

Callie eased her back to a trot and then a walk well away from the pen's railing.

Glow tossed her head and danced, knowing she'd done well.

Callie ripped her hat off and tossed it into the air, whooping. "We did it."

"Well done." Brody clapped.

Callie started and spun in the saddle to see him resting his forearms on the gate.

One side of his mouth turned up in a grin.

She'd missed that smile the most over the years. The one that said he was proud of her.

Chapter Eight

Callie spent most of Friday in the barn. Between working the gray mare and riding Glow, her day had passed faster than any so far. She retreated to Tenley's at four to clean up.

Tenley met her at the door and dragged her inside. "Remember that favor I asked you for?"

Callie nearly tripped over a pile of fabrics and a tote that spilled ribbons—and something that looked suspiciously like a textbook on equine therapy—across the floor. Tenley had been on a crafting kick all week. Her house looked like a tiny carnival. Every nook and cranny held some object she'd put together for the auction. Callie righted herself and tucked a bottle of glue back into the clear tote where it belonged.

She brushed hair from her eyes and moved toward her bedroom. "The rodeo? I remember, but I still don't know what you're wanting me to do. I can't organize an event like that."

Tenley hesitated before following.

Callie gathered up clean clothes and faced the bathroom.

Tenley blocked the door and gave Callie a cautious

look. What was that about? Tenley sighed and twisted her hands into a knot. "Okay, look. I asked Brody to talk to Mr. Wells about hosting the rodeo. You're going with him tonight to pick up Luke's horse."

"I fail to see what one has to do with the other." She wanted a shower to wash away the grime. Food to fill the empty space in her stomach. No time for either. The last thing she needed was to be late meeting Brody.

He'd not wait for her.

"I'm afraid Brody won't ask him. Mr. Wells, I mean. Brody is set against this entire thing. It's like he believes the town will think less of us because we're in debt." Tenley rolled her eyes. "My brother has his head stuck in the sand, and he's not coming up anytime soon. He'd rather we lose the ranch than admit he needs help."

Callie knew the old Brody well enough to realize Tenley spoke the truth. Even as a teen, he'd been adamant that he functioned best alone. It was one of his most annoying qualities.

She'd almost married him. What would have happened then? How did a marriage work when one party thought themselves above asking for help?

"I need you to talk to Mr. Wells. If Brody brings it up, great. If he doesn't, will you?"

Oh, no. She was not getting in the middle of a Jacobs family feud. Callie started to shake her head. "I remember telling you that if something put me and Brody at odds, then I wouldn't do it." She eased past Tenley and shut the door.

"Please, Callie. We need this."

Callie remained silent.

"Can I at least put your name on the poster? If people

know *the* Calamity Jane is coming, then we're bound to have a good turnout."

"Fine," she called through the door. "As long as the rodeo happens before I leave."

The faster she got out of here, the better.

Her heart already wanted to attach itself to this family. It almost felt like she'd never left. They loved and accepted her. No hard feelings. No recriminations. No guilt except what she put on herself.

Why couldn't her own parents love her like Margaret and Peter?

She showered and changed while ruminating on her parents. They'd been absent from her life for so long that she hardly remembered them. Her father had showed up at a rodeo in Tucson a year ago and they'd run into each other by accident.

She'd stopped telling them her route years ago. Callie nibbled her lip and retrieved her phone. Would they come now if she told them what she was attempting? Did she want them there to see her potentially fail?

No. Better to let them hear of it through the rodeo channels.

Callie exited the bathroom and darted into the kitchen.

Tenley stood at the kitchen table. Her shoulders shook as tears ran down her cheeks.

Regret landed heavy on Callie's shoulders. When had Tenley ever asked her for anything? Never that Callie could remember. While she worried over whether her parents would bother to show up at a rodeo, Tenley was fighting to help save her family's ranch.

Callie thought she'd gotten over her selfishness. She'd been blind to her faults for a long time. No more. "I'll talk to him."

"It's okay. You don't have to." Her voice quivered.

Callie looped her arms around Tenley and squeezed. "If he doesn't agree, I'll talk to my sponsors. They might be willing to help. No promises. Todd is a hard-nosed workaholic. I'm pretty sure he's a good guy. Deep down. We'll pray Mr. Wells agrees. He's a better option."

"Thanks."

"Anything for the Jacobses." Callie squeezed again then backed away. "I need to go meet Brody."

"Hey, Callie, you ready to go?" Brody's voice leaked through the front door. He knocked and twisted the knob. "Tenley, you home?"

"Come in." Tenley dabbed at her puffy eyes.

Brody entered. If he knew Tenley had been crying, he didn't say anything. He wore his expressionless mask today. The all-work posture locked his shoulders back and put a scowl on his lips.

He stopped at the boxes of ribbon and tucked his hands into his pockets. "It's five."

"Well, then I guess we should get going." A hope to put Brody off his game worked its way in. Callie didn't let herself resist. "And we should grab dinner on the way."

Brody's stride faltered as he turned away. "Sure. Dinner. Why don't we swing by Granny's on our way through town and grab some burgers?"

"Sounds great."

She tossed him the keys and a half hour later, he wheeled her six-horse trailer into the parking lot across from Granny's, a fifties-era diner that was a staple of downtown Tamarack Springs.

They dropped to the pavement and slammed doors in simultaneous thuds. Callie's stomach grumbled, reminding her she'd skipped breakfast and lunch in favor of spending her time with the horses.

Brody pulled the door open and held it for Callie to precede him into the black-and-white-tiled lounge. Red stools lined the bar. Red booths spread out along both front windows. She remembered the scarred tables and the way light filtered through the windows to cast the kitchen in a honeyed glow.

It smelled of grease and ketchup. Old memories roared to life, tugging insistently at her memory.

Granny herself shuffled from behind the counter and waved her wooden spoon at them. "Brody, good to see you. And who's that?" She squinted and whacked the spoon on the counter. "As I live and breathe, Callie Wade. Is that you?" She hustled forward, apron tight over her waist and hips swaying. Her orthopedic shoes slapped the tiles. Customers spun on their stools and gaped as Granny threw her arms around Callie and hauled her down to the older woman's four-foot-nine stature.

She squeezed Callie's neck until her eyes bugged. "Can't breathe, Granny." The woman had the arms of a steel trap.

"Right. Sorry, dear." Granny let go long enough to pinch Callie's cheeks and nudge her and Brody to the right. "Go on, grab a booth. What'll you have?"

"Granny, I'll take their order." A young woman wearing a flattering apron covered in pastel swirls pulled a pad and paper from her pocket. "What'll you have?"

"Burger and fries," Callie answered while sliding into the booth.

Brody nodded. "Same for me."

The woman slipped away, scribbling on her notepad.

Granny shook her head and tsked. "Good girl, that Tess. She's my granddaughter. Did you know that, Callie?"

"I remember." Tess was a few years younger than Callie, but they'd not been close friends. "We rode in the pony club together."

"That's right." Granny tapped her spoon on the table. "You still ride, don't you? My great-grandson has been begging for a pony." She faced Brody. "You selling any of yours?"

"Not right now. Still training." Brody left it there and Granny seemed to understand.

After she walked away, Callie spoke. "You still want to raise and train your own horses?"

"Someday."

"You're going to look up one day and find out that someday slipped by. You could start with one horse. Are any of the horses at the ranch yours?"

"The gelding you rode on the trail ride."

Callie pursed her lips and waited while Tess put down twin glasses of sweet tea. In Granny's, everyone got sweet tea with their meals. You could order anything you wanted. You'd get tea. Granny didn't believe in anything else except water and coffee and she only served coffee at breakfast.

"You still want to raise foals from Glow?" He tore the paper from his straw and tossed it at her. It bounced on the table and into her lap.

Callie swept it into her palm and deposited it beside her own. "I did." She sipped her tea. "But how would I sell them? Who's going to want a foal with a degenerative eye disease that could show up at any time?"

"From a 1D barrel racer like Glow, you're talking half the rodeo population. The risk of disease is low, and even if it did strike, you're looking at years in the arena or doing whatever their riders wish. Years of love and care. If you'd known about Glow from the day she was born, would you have picked another horse?" He raised his eyebrows, the challenge obvious in his gaze.

She'd never thought about it like that.

The food arrived, giving Callie time to gather her fractured thoughts. Not that she needed long. Brody's question had a simple answer; it merely clogged her throat to consider she might need to retire the horse that had given Callie every win of her career. And every defeat. She and Glow had been inseparable since the day she'd realized Glow's potential. It sounded clinical. Like she only wanted Glow because of the potential to win, but they were a team. When everything else went wrong, Glow was still there.

Callie had walked away from every person she'd loved, but she'd taken Glow with her. Glow was the one she counted on to always be there, and soon she'd be forced to give that up. Her horse's career as a barrel racer ticked down each day. They were getting too old for the rodeo.

Callie picked at her fries and found Brody staring at her through the clouds of steam rising from their burgers. "I wouldn't trade Glow for the most expensive barrel racer on the circuit. Past or present."

He shot her a grin.

"How's the food?" Granny returned and refilled their tea.

"Fabulous." Callie shoved in another fry.

Brody eyed Callie as they rolled into Mr. Wells's drive. She stared out the window, a pensive look pinching her eyes. Their talk ceased once they'd left Granny's, and he couldn't say he regretted the silence.

They stepped out of the truck at the same time. Sunlight dappled the fields and cast long shadows that edged toward Brody's boots.

Daniel moved from the door of the barn and waved. "Nice night for a drive."

Yes, it certainly was, not that Brody had noticed until the man brought it to his attention. He inhaled the scents of fresh-mowed grass and horse. No hiding the smells of a place that housed what looked like over two dozen horses.

"Had any luck finding homes for the other horses?"

Daniel shrugged his shoulders. "Most of these are stabled here. Owners pay me to feed and care for them. They come by and ride from time to time."

Explained how he kept the place going. Training. Teaching. Stabling. Seemed the man had his hands in all the equine arenas.

Callie paced to the fence and propped her arms on the white rail. Ranger flicked his tail and nosed her arm. Her shoulders lowered and the tightness in her eyes eased. What worried her mind to the point that the frown lines had become almost a permanent feature? The only time she relaxed was when she worked with the horses.

Daniel chuckled. "That girl loves horses."

"Don't they all?" Brody shifted his weight and cleared his throat. He needed to do the job he came here for.

Tenley's request from the day before lodged in his throat. His shoulders tightened and the words stuck.

He couldn't do it. His sister wanted too much from him. Tenley could take care of the fundraiser.

"Thank you for holding Ranger for us. You didn't have to do that." It felt like the right thing to say. Brody sucked air through his teeth. "We'd best get him loaded and get out of here."

"Your nephew is one lucky kid." Daniel moved toward Callie. "You give any more thought to my offer?"

Too much. Brody rolled his shoulders to ease the tightness gathering across his entire body. "I appreciate you thinking of me." He took a moment to look around. Pristine buildings surrounded by perfect fences and horses. It was more than he could handle. "I've worked too long and too hard to compromise now."

The man frowned until creases appeared in his cheeks. "This place is not settling. You'd have access to my entire client base. Facilities of the highest quality." He stared hard at Brody. "I suppose I'm curious why you're so opposed to coming on as my head trainer."

"I'd be answering to you. I've never had to answer to anyone before."

"Not even God?"

Brody jolted, feeling like he'd grabbed an electric fence on full voltage.

Callie patted Ranger and slipped between the rails to check over the gelding.

What gave this man the right to question Brody's faith? He opened his mouth to say exactly that when the look on the older man's face caused Brody's breath to leave in a rush. The weight of his dad's surgeries, the debt, the ranch, it all suddenly felt like too much.

He was collapsing under the burden God had put on his shoulders. To give it up now seemed like admitting he wasn't capable of bearing what God had given him charge over.

Allowing the people of Tamarack Springs to pay for his family's debt hurt his pride.

Pain shot through his heart. Pride.

One of his worst enemies. How many times had his family accused him of having too much pride? He'd ignored their jabs, shoving them aside as nothing more than their jealousy.

What if they were right?

Daniel took a step back. "If you change your mind, you know where I am."

Brody realized then that he'd been standing silent and staring at Callie.

He'd made up his mind when the man had first called. "Thank you again for the horse."

"Sure, son." Daniel followed Brody to the rail.

Brody passed Callie the lead rope he'd retrieved from the trailer.

Callie clipped the lead onto the horse's halter and led him toward the gate.

Daniel met her there and trailed a hand down Ranger's side as the horse walked out. "Have a good life, old man." Emotion tinged his tone and his voice quivered.

Brody understood. It had taken all his strength to give up his old horse, Mischief, but it had been necessary. He'd make the same decision again. Giving up what he wanted for his family came as second nature after all these years.

"You're frowning." Callie tapped his arm. "Why are you frowning? This is a happy day."

"It seems I've given your Brody a sour apple by inviting him to work here." The man didn't cut corners when he spoke.

Callie continued toward the trailer, her gaze darting

side to side. She already knew about the offer, thanks to his parents.

Brody's scowl deepened. Why did everyone come at him all at once? "I'm sorry that I can't help you. Really. This job just isn't for me."

"Training…" Callie trailed off. Her eyebrows were up and her nostrils flaring.

If she were a horse, he'd know that expression meant he'd better watch out.

From Callie, it meant she longed to call his bluff. Ten years ago, she would not have hesitated. A beat of tense silence passed before Callie shook her head. "You amaze me, Brody. You say you want to train world-class horses but then turn down the job that gives you what you asked for."

"I can't leave my barn to drive here every day. Why save the ranch at all if I'm not even going to use it?" The words poured from him. Once he'd released the stopper on his thoughts, it refused to go back. "The Triple Bar Ranch is my home. It's what I've been fighting for all these years."

"Moving to something else doesn't make you a quitter," Callie interjected before he could delve any deeper into his emotions.

He'd thank her if he wasn't so angry. He knocked his hat off his head and slapped it against his leg. "It's settling for less than my dream. I've already done that once." When she'd left and he'd stayed behind, he'd lost his dream. Never again.

Callie's eyes hardened into blue chips. Her jaw jutted forward. Another warning. She led Ranger into the trailer, hooked him to the tie and stomped down the ramp. She stopped in front of Daniel and gave Brody one last look. "Did Brody ask you about the rodeo?"

Brody felt his heart plummet to his toes.

"Rodeo?" He shook his head side to side. "We were busy discussing Brody not coming to work here. I'm afraid he didn't have time to mention a rodeo."

Sweet of the old man to cover for Brody, but the lie scorched through him. "I had no intention of asking you." Shame added its weight to his shoulders.

"Brody." Callie's quiet admonition raised his gaze to her face. Sorrow carved shadows into her eyes. Her warm fingers wrapped around his arm. "Stop." She blinked and a tear tracked down her cheek. "Please stop trying to do this alone. It isn't weakness to need help."

"I don't need help."

"Maybe you don't, but your father does. Your mother does. Tenley and Molly want to help. This is a great thing and they're doing it to take the weight from you." She took a step closer.

Their breaths crashed together. She stood near enough, he saw the starburst of gold around her irises. "Let us in."

The world froze. Brody took a step back, breaking the spell.

Daniel cleared his throat.

Brody jolted at the sound. He'd forgotten the man was standing there.

Callie's face fell and Brody recognized the disappointment even as she faced the man. "Brody's family is having a fundraising rodeo for his dad's surgery. I'll be taking care of setting up barrel racing and other events, but we need a place to hold the event. Brody's sister, Tenley, looked you up. I'm afraid that's my fault. I told her how beautiful it is here."

Indignation flooded Brody's veins. He'd inquired why Tenley had refused to have the rodeo at the Triple Bar. She'd said it wasn't enough of an attention grabber. And they didn't have the proper facilities.

All valid points.

Daniel smiled so wide, it had to pinch his cheeks. "I've heard Peter's story. I'd be honored to give you full access to the main barn, the arena and the training facilities on either hill."

Brody heard Callie's breath catch. No doubt this was more than she'd expected.

The man handed out his ranch like it didn't even matter to him anymore.

Come on, Brody. You're acting jealous.

He was jealous.

He pushed down the rush of annoyance. He'd been called out on basically every bad habit he possessed. His dad would be disappointed.

Brody disappointed himself. Is this really the man he'd become?

The fundraiser was happening with or without him. "I'm sorry I didn't bring it up. I'd like to say that I forgot, but I didn't." He ran a hand through his hair and twisted the hat in his clenched fist. "I'll give you the honest truth. I don't think we need this fundraiser." He dug his heels in harder than an untrained colt.

"Good thing it isn't your decision to make." Callie turned and flounced toward the passenger door. "I'll have Tenley call and set everything up. I'll need to come by a few days ahead of time to help."

Daniel eyed Brody. His smile remained in place despite the tempestuous conversation. "Take care, Brody."

"You, too, Mr. Wells."

He pushed out a hand. "Daniel. Please call me Daniel."

Brody coughed. "I need to get this guy home and hidden in the barn." He lifted his eyes to the setting sun. They had minutes of daylight left. He'd need to text Molly and ensure Luke was kept busy when the trailer rolled in.

One flash of headlights or the squeak of a hinge and Luke would ruin his own birthday surprise.

Brody hopped into the cab and pointed them toward home.

Callie sat in her seat, arms and legs crossed. Her foot jigged up and down.

Uh-oh. She gave off warning signals stronger than a surly colt.

"Go ahead and say it."

"Say what?" Her foot jigged faster. "I'm not part of your family anymore. It isn't my place to say anything."

"You are part of this family." Whether he liked it or not. "You think if I had taken off for ten years I'd be kicked out? It doesn't work that way. Not even for an honorary Jacobs."

Callie used her palms to wipe her face. "That's not fair. I was all set to be mad at you the whole drive home. You go and say stuff like that, and I can't stay mad."

Brody's grip on the wheel tightened. She'd called the ranch home.

No. He would not let that little slip of hers persuade him to reconsider his change in feelings. Loving Callie was off-limits.

Chapter Nine

Callie never should've agreed to the birthday party. Coming back to the ranch was a mistake. Every day she spent here made it harder to think about leaving. Too late to back out. She tucked the gift under her arm and knocked on Molly's door.

She hadn't needed to ask where the party was being held. The balloons tied all around the porch posts, not to mention the banner draped across the front door, drew Callie in. Her knock went unanswered. Callie shifted from foot to foot and knocked again.

"Might as well go on in." Brody's voice snapped her around.

Spinning, she clutched the gift to her stomach. "Brody. What are you doing here? I mean I thought you'd be inside already."

"Nope. Waiting for the right moment to show up."

"Were you watching me?"

His smile sent butterflies fluttering.

Molly snapped open the door and urged them into the house, where chaos ensued in the form of children running amok.

A little girl careened into the door and Callie caught her before she tumbled to the floor.

Brody hiked his shoulder and puffed his cheeks. "Well, this'll be fun."

"When are you giving him Ranger?"

Molly shushed Callie with a hissing breath. "Later. After the kids leave. If we do it now, we'll never get him back to the house to spend time with his friends."

"I promised to give him a lesson today. Is that still okay?" She dropped Luke's gift onto a table filled to bursting. Colorful paper fluttered in the air-conditioned breeze.

"Absolutely. It's all he talked about this morning."

Callie sidestepped a pair of kids playing hopscotch across the living room and followed Molly into the kitchen. A cake sat on the counter. Three tiers of midnight blue with stars sprinkled around the top. Horses galloped around each tier, their details perfect enough they might leap from the cake at any moment.

Brody whistled. "Wow, Molls. Best one yet."

Callie's mouth popped open. "You made this?"

"You should see what she did for the Smith wedding last winter." Brody slung an arm around Molly's shoulders and attempted to swipe at the icing.

She batted his hand away. "Stop that."

"Seriously." Brody faced Callie, but the words seemed to be for Molly alone. "You need to get your bakery up and running."

Callie searched his face for any indication that he wanted to convince Molly to back out of the fundraiser. She found nothing but support for his sister.

Molly grinned as a rabble rose from the back porch. Laughter filled the house and dove into Callie's heart.

She loved kids. Their laughter and sheer joy always brightened her mood.

Molly slid a cream-colored envelope toward Brody. "The bakery might be closer than I thought."

He flipped the envelope open and extracted a thick invitation. He read quickly then passed the paper to Callie while he smiled and drew Molly into a hug. "Congratulations, kiddo."

"It isn't official. They liked my video. That's all." But Molly's smile rivaled her son's as he sailed into the room and climbed onto a chair to stare at his cake.

"Can we eat it?" He inched forward.

Molly eyed the clock. "Sure. Cake time." She ushered Luke from the room. "Brody, get the candles. Luke, let's gather your friends."

Callie read the invitation while Brody moved around the kitchen. "An invitation to present a cake for consideration in the Baker's Blessing Baking Bonanza." She frowned, slid the paper into the envelope, and returned it to the basket beside Molly's keys and cell phone. "What's a baking bonanza?"

"Molly's chance to earn the money to purchase a building outright instead of borrowing the money." Brody found a package of candles and paced to the table. "She's earned the right to live her dream. I just wish there was a way I could help."

Tenley darted in. "Oh, come on, Brody. You can't keep us all afloat. What about your dreams? Don't you deserve to see yours realized?"

"I have enough." His eyes dropped, the color going hard as gemstones.

Callie knew better. He'd admitted as much. He still wanted to train those famous horses. To be a trainer the world respected. She opened her mouth to say as much when a cascade of children tumbled into the room.

Brody caught her eye and she thought she saw relief etched there as the conversation ended.

Peter rolled in behind the kids, roaring and chasing them as they screamed and scrambled onto chairs.

Margaret gave Brody an indulgent smile and hurried to pull ice cream from the freezer.

Callie made her way to a corner, where she could watch the party without interfering. The family worked as a unit. Molly helped the kids sit while Tenley organized plates and forks. Brody stuck five candles into the top tier of the cake and then stepped back.

A rousing rendition of "Happy Birthday" blasted off-key and out of sync. Laughter sounded as the singing slowed. Molly lit the candles and helped Luke lean close enough to blow out the flames.

"I'm five now." Luke clapped and hopped across the room, going to join his friends.

The rest of the party passed in a blur of cake, ice cream and enough laughter that Callie's sides ached. She stepped outside to answer her ringing phone and barely managed a hello before Sam launched into a rapid-fire stream of questions. "Where are you, Callie? Have you seen what's happening on the circuit? You need to get back here."

"Slow down, Sam. What's going on?"

"Everyone's saying you'll never race again. There's a rumor, no one knows where it started or with who, but they're saying Glow's done. That you left and either you won't be back or that Glow's a washed-up pony who's lost her gumption to run." Sam's voice cracked, but Callie knew better than to think Sam felt any remorse for the tales. If anything, she'd started them herself. But then why would she call and tell Callie...unless she thought it would put doubt in her mind.

"Glow's fine. I'm fine. We'll be back in a few more weeks."

"If you and Glow are fine, then why aren't you back yet? It's been two weeks. Glow isn't yours, Callie. You owe me a phone call, at the very least, to update me on her progress. Has the vet been out to check her leg?"

"It's fine. The sprain is healed. We're resting up and getting ready."

"Callie, I bought Glow from you as a favor. That doesn't mean you get to leave with her and not tell me where you are. They might not hang horse thieves any-more, but taking off with someone else's horse is still frowned upon." The sound of stomping drifted through from Sam's side, followed by the rasp of a stall door sliding open. "Where did you take Glow, and what's really going on?"

"You saw that fall, Sam. We needed a little time to recuperate." Callie chewed her lip. She needed to keep her location a secret for a little while longer. "I need Glow in tip-top shape if I'm going to beat you in the next rodeo and buy her back."

"Ha. Good luck with that." Sam's competitive spirit kicked in and she gusted out a sigh. "I have to know where you are, Callie. It's my responsibility as Glow's owner. I don't want to be mean, but I don't have to let you ride her. You know that, right? That mare is seventy percent mine."

"But our contract says that I'm her rider. Doesn't matter how many shares you have. You can't give her to another rider."

"Unless that rider is me."

Callie's stomach dropped. "No."

"Yes. It's in the contract, Callie. I'm not saying I'm taking Glow away from you. I have my own horse, and we're going to stomp you and that flashy palomino into the ground in two weeks, but I need a release from the vet first and I can't get one if I don't know where you are."

Two weeks? Callie had thought she and Glow still had a month with Brody. She shook her head. Sam must have gotten her dates messed up.

"What if I get the vet here to send you a release?" Surely, that would be enough.

"No. It's the rodeo vet or nothing. And nothing means you don't ride."

Callie still hesitated. She pinched the bridge of her nose to keep the rush of tears at bay. "I brought her home. To Tamarack Springs."

Silence rang from Sam's side of the phone.

Callie waited. Sam never stayed quiet for long. She'd have something to say, Callie had no doubt.

"That single-stoplight town where I found you?" A gusty laugh. "That's where you are? You're not staying, are you?"

Luke ran past, streamers flying in his wake and a dozen kids on his trail.

Callie's stomach tightened and her grip on the phone eased as she followed Luke. Molly and Brody headed off the horde, guiding them to the backyard. Callie followed at a distance and found the fenced-in yard overflowing with all manner of play equipment.

"Callie?" Sam's voice dimmed the joy brightening the day.

Callie shook her head. "I have to go, Sam. I made a little boy a promise that I intend to keep."

She joined the others at the fence and listened as parents began gathering up their children. Luke waved goodbye and ran to Molly the minute the last kid left the yard. "Can we see my horse now?"

"Luke, I never said you were getting a horse." Molly glanced at Brody.

"But I am." His quiet assurance plucked at Callie's heartstrings. How did anyone turn down faith like that? Luke took his mother by the hand and pulled her toward the barn. "Coming, Uncle Brody?"

"Right behind you, champ." Brody took Peter's hand and squeezed.

Peter nodded and wiped tears from his eyes. "Let's hurry. Don't want to miss this." He wheeled to the barn, his hands flashing across the wheelchair too quick for Callie to follow.

She stayed back, keeping out of the ring of family.

Margaret glanced back and frowned. "Hurry, Callie." She waved and the heaviness dogging Callie's steps eased. Her emotions rode a roller coaster of highs and lows. One minute she felt on top of the world, then she remembered her imminent departure and it came crashing down.

What would have happened if she'd told Sam no that night in Granny's when the woman had offered to help Callie break into the rodeo circuit?

With her and Brody working together, would they have managed to pay off the debt in time for them to both achieve their dreams?

Brody laughed at something Tenley said, the sound teasing a smile from Callie against her will. He was happy here. Dreams achieved or not, Brody had found a way to be content. When was the last time she'd felt anything beyond the rush of a good run?

Peter beat them all to the barn and waited inside. Molly lifted her phone and tapped a few buttons before giving Brody a nod. "Okay. Let's do this."

Brody dropped to a knee and put a hand on Luke's shoulder. "Can you stay here for a minute?"

Luke nodded, sending his cowboy hat listing to one side.

The horses leaned over their stall doors, watching with ears pricked as Brody walked past.

Callie held her breath when he slid open the stall door at the end of the barn and reached inside.

Luke clapped his hands over his eyes.

"You can look, Luke." Tenley nudged him with her knee, but the little boy shook his head.

His voice quivered as his hands tightened over his face. "Not yet."

Ranger seemed to know there was something special about this moment. He lifted his head and walked quietly by Brody's side. His hooves stirred the hay and sent dust motes swirling into the sunlight streaming through the barn.

Luke swallowed hard and dropped his hands.

Callie waited, they all seemed to hold their breath.

Luke burst into tears. "He's perfect."

Brody stopped Ranger a handful of steps away from Luke, and the little boy wiped his cheeks. Tears continued streaming. Ranger dropped his head, snuffled Luke's hat, then bumped his nose into Luke's shoulder.

Callie's heart thumped as Luke wrapped his arms around Ranger's head and held on for dear life.

Molly's hands shook so hard that Callie doubted she'd be able to see anything of the video she recorded.

Tears dampened Callie's cheeks. Like Luke, she dashed them away and plucked the phone from Molly's hands. "Go. I'll do this."

Molly shot her a grateful smile and reached down to hug Luke. He threw his arms around her neck. "Thank you, Mama."

"You're welcome."

Tenley sniffled beside Callie but no tears fell. Too much like her brother to show emotion in front of the others, Tenley gripped her elbows and smiled. Her chin wobbled, but she held the tears at bay. "That's what it's all about." She glanced at Callie, heart shining through her eyes.

Callie agreed.

Luke spun on his heel. "Can you teach us now, Callie?"

They all burst into laughter.

Callie passed the phone back to Molly. "Yes. I can teach you now. Let's get him saddled up."

The little boy whooped and spun in a circle. Laughter filled the barn and Ranger tossed his head up and down like he agreed with his owner's enthusiasm.

Callie headed out to the small arena to wait while Brody helped his nephew saddle the gelding.

They walked out together, Luke leading the horse and the others trailing behind. He climbed into the saddle and grinned at Callie. "We're ready. Can we run in the rodeo?"

Rodeo? What rodeo? Callie shifted her gaze to Molly, but the woman was busy recording Luke's first ride.

"The rodeo at the Wellses' ranch." Tenley lowered

her hands to the middle rail and gripped it tight. "The one you and Brody are helping me set up."

Oh. That rodeo. Callie resisted the urge to pull at her shirt collar to ease the tightness. She'd practically forgotten about the fundraiser despite talking to Daniel Wells yesterday.

Her attention returned to Luke. She had a job to do right here. The planning for the rodeo would wait another day.

Brody settled into a hard plastic chair on Monday morning and rolled a cup of coffee between his palms. His family fanned the room, spreading out on either side of him. They were in for a long wait, despite his dad being the first on the surgery schedule this morning.

White walls closed in.

"What a way to start a Monday." Tenley downed her coffee and strode toward the machine where more percolated. They'd already emptied the first pot and had started another. Tenley tapped her cup, the sound beating through the waiting room like rain on a tin roof. "Who wants snacks?"

"Tenley, we just got here." Molly leaned her head on the wall and stared at the television anchored high in the far corner. A game show played on silent, making the expressions on the people's faces comical despite the chill air and antiseptic smell permeating the room.

Tenley shifted from boot to boot, never able to stand still for more than a handful of minutes. "I'm a nervous eater. Dad's in surgery. We're stuck here with nothing to do. I want sweets." She shoved a hand into her pocket and came up with a handful of change. "I'm going to find a vending machine. Who wants chocolate?"

"Me." Callie strode into the room, bringing a rush of coconut and pineapple to push away the blistering scent of alcohol and paper tape. She passed Brody and settled in the chair across from him.

Brody straightened from his stooped position, retreating from Callie's closeness. Guilt followed. He was in a hospital waiting room. Now was not the time to be having feelings for Callie. He gulped the coffee, burning his tongue in the process, and grimaced at the bitter liquid. "Hope all the coffee doesn't taste this bad."

"I'll get you some of the good stuff while I'm exploring." Tenley took a wad of dollar bills from Molly and gave what passed as a smile when confronted by the realization that their father wasn't invincible.

It tangled Brody's stomach into knots. He didn't know how Tenley managed to eat anything, much less sugary sweets. He barely managed to hold down the coffee. Anything solid was out of the question. His foot bounced on the tile and he developed a sudden urge to chew his fingernails.

Thankfully, she hadn't brought up the fundraiser in a few days. He'd managed to avoid admitting his inability to ask Daniel about the rodeo. He eyed Callie. Had she told Tenley?

"Brody, what's that game you used to play?" Molly draped her arms over the chair and stretched. Her eyebrows lowered into slashes. She looked ready to take on however many hours this day threw her way. "The one you and Callie would spend hours laughing over." She gave him a look that said she needed a distraction. They all did.

Mom had sat down after the surgeon left and hadn't moved since. Brody watched her for a beat before Molly's question registered. "Divide and Conquer." He glanced at Callie, who stared back at him with wide eyes.

"What do you do? You never let us play."

"You imagine a perfect scenario, then your opponent attempts to grant your scenario while also ruining it." He forced his leg to stop bouncing. "For example, I once said I would be the best horse trainer in the world. Callie said I'd be the best horse trainer but I'd only train one horse for the rest of my life."

Tenley returned, her arms loaded with candy bars and a tray of coffees that wobbled as she nudged the door shut behind her. "Oh, Divide and Conquer. I love that game."

"You got to play?" Molly glared at Brody. "You never let me play."

"You were too young. All you wanted was a cake." Brody took a coffee from Tenley and relaxed into his seat. "We felt bad for always ruining your cake."

Callie took the remote and flipped the TV to another channel. She paused, leaving the station on the local rodeo.

Brody watched as she stiffened and crossed her arms. Her eyes narrowed and she focused on the screen. Was she missing the rodeo? If anything, her expression told him she'd rather be anywhere else. He attributed that to their current situation holed up in a hospital waiting room.

They'd all rather be anywhere else. In the saddle sounded perfect right now.

Tenley moved to stand beside Callie, the two of them creating a contrast of blond and brown braids. They were of matching height, but Callie had a leanness built into her from years with the rodeo. Tenley shifted her coffee to her left hand and bit into a candy bar. "Who're you rooting for?" She jabbed the coffee at the screen when Callie raised her brows. "If you can't win, who do you root for?"

"Sam." Callie answered without hesitation, but Brody caught a lilt in her voice that almost made it sound like a question.

Tenley grimaced. "You don't have to root for your partner." She bit off another hunk of chocolate. "Is it hard competing against her?"

Brody stiffened, his hand clamping on the cup until it crumpled in his grip. He leaned into Callie's answer. Questions burned the back of his throat. She'd admitted why she'd really left, but what about the years in between? Had she missed them? He thought so. Her lingering glances filled his mind. She moved around the barn like she belonged there, like she'd never left. But she never seemed to let herself get completely comfortable.

"Sam and I are not what you'd call friends. We're competitors who have the same sponsors, and she's helped me out of some tight situations." Callie raised a shoulder and exhaled. The words were soft and quick.

Brody couldn't help but feel like she was keeping something from them.

Hours passed, each one longer than the last. By the time the doctor came into the room to inform them that Dad was in recovery and doing well, Brody had ingested enough coffee to make a trucker proud.

The Jacobs siblings gathered up their belongings and hurried to their dad's room. Dr. Blythe held open the door. "You have five minutes."

Five minutes to settle all their nerves before they

made the trek home. Dad was still groggy from the anesthesia, so Brody left quickly and headed home, where he parked beside the barn. Mom was staying at the hospital overnight with Dad. Tenley and Molly were taking turns keeping Mom company once they gathered the necessary items of distraction. For Tenley, that meant card games and more coffee. For Molly, a stack of baking magazines. She and Mom could sit all night discussing recipes while Dad slept.

"I'm so glad the surgery was a success." Callie popped up beside his truck window and gripped the sill.

Brody nodded, unable to answer for the sting behind his eyes. The doctor said the spinal fusion had become necessary to keep the vertebrae from rubbing on the spinal cord and doing further damage. It was frightening how fragile the human body was. God had done something wonderful in His creation. But it was so easily destroyed.

"I'm going to check on Glow. Need me to work any of the horses?"

Brody eyed the sky. Dusk approached, giving them a few hours of daylight, but he couldn't bring himself to work. If he wasn't willing, he'd not ask Callie to work in his place. "Take the day off. You've earned it."

Callie beamed, though fatigue ringed her eyes. He didn't doubt his own face looked haggard after their morning, but he slid from the truck and breathed in the smell of home.

He followed Callie into the barn and began his chores. No matter how tired he felt or how his body complained, stalls didn't muck themselves and the feed troughs didn't fill on their own.

Maybe if he worked for Daniel Wells, he would have

others to do this work. He'd be free to focus on the training.

What would that be like?

Brody shook the thought away. It made no difference. He'd bent far enough to stop fighting the fundraiser. That was enough.

Callie murmured from inside Glow's stall. Her voice pitched high then low.

Brody frowned and took a step closer.

Callie leaned across Glow's withers, cell phone pressed to her ear. "You promised."

Whatever the caller said caused Callie's frown to deepen. She leaned her head on Glow's back, the image of dejection.

Several tense seconds passed before she straightened.

Brody spun on his heel, hoping to keep from being caught eavesdropping. Not that he'd heard anything anyway.

Callie's footsteps hit the concrete aisle. "Brody, wait."

He stopped as his heart dropped. He knew that tone. It was the same one she'd used the night she'd left.

Callie pulled her braid over her shoulder and twisted it into a knot, a sure sign of her nervousness. She looked at him and blinked. Her gaze slid away. "That was my sponsor."

"Let me guess, another ad." Her sponsors were driving him to distraction by hauling her away every week. How did they expect him to get any work done? "We'll never get Glow ready if you're constantly taking off."

"They want me to ride." She shook her head and her mouth pinched into a flat line. "No. They demand I meet up with Sam in Arizona and ride Maverick."

Maverick? Brody rolled the name around. "What

about your whole thing about not riding any horse except Glow?"

"I tried to tell Todd, but he refused to listen. It's that contract." She tugged on her braid and growled. "I never should have signed. Worst decision ever."

That meant that leaving him probably took second place. Way to shoot an arrow straight to his heart.

"Tell him you have work to do here. Stand up for Glow."

"I don't have a choice, Brody. If I don't ride, they'll pull my sponsorship. That means no last ride with Glow. We'll go out as the pair that crashed and burned." A hard glint entered her eyes. "I won't let that be our legacy."

Anger surged and collided with disappointment. He was too tired—too emotionally drained—to dampen his voice. "Go then." He waved a hand at the open fields beyond the barn. He was being unfair. He knew it but couldn't stop.

"This isn't what I want."

"Then fight for it." He kicked at the dirt and jerked his Stetson from his head. "Fight for what you want." His throat closed. A war waged between his emotions. "Stay." The single word forced its way out.

"I can't." Tears pooled and her breaths grew ragged. She took a step forward, putting them inches apart. "One more ride. That's all I'm asking for. That's what I'm fighting for."

"If you don't stay with Glow, she'll never be ready in time." *Stay.* It pulsed in his heart, beating in time and rushing through every inhale. He'd wanted few things in his life with this kind of need.

Her throat dipped in an audible swallow. "I'll be back, and we'll train harder than ever." She made it sound like a promise.

But he knew better than to trust her promises. He supposed this moment had been a long time coming. His anger drained away. Callie wanted to live her dream.

"I won't stand in your way then." Exhaustion curved his shoulders. He turned his back on the only woman he'd ever loved. If he didn't, he might grab her and try to hold on to an impossible future. "I'll do what I can with Glow while you're gone."

Callie fled the barn without a backward glance. The night from ten years ago replayed in his mind as she ran.

Brody rubbed his chest. The pain lingered, piercing hot and cold. He'd started to fall for her again. After all this time and all the baggage between them, he had given her the benefit of the doubt. He'd trusted her and she'd stabbed him in the heart. Again.

When would he learn his lesson? *Help me, Lord. I can't keep doing this.* He sent the prayer heavenward and closed his eyes. Would God give him the peace he needed to let her go?

Callie Wade would never stick around when he needed her.

It was past time he stopped needing her. It proved his point that the only person he could rely on was himself. And God.

Callie's truck engine fired up. Gravel spun under her wheels with the force of her acceleration.

He'd angered her. Good.

Ranger bobbed his head at Brody and wiggled his lip. Three days and Luke had the horse spoiled rotten.

Brody groaned. The rodeo was scheduled for the following weekend. Callie hadn't bothered telling him how long she would be gone.

That meant he'd be the one responsible for setting up the event and rounding up people and horses.

He dialed Tenley's number and retreated to the feed room. He'd wasted enough time waiting on Callie. Time to get back to work and put all this behind him once and for all.

When Callie came back for Glow, he'd load the mare up and say goodbye forever. No more looking back and hoping for a different future.

No more Callie hovering on the edges of his mind or anchoring in his heart.

I trusted that she came back for a reason. Why did it all go wrong? Brody slipped the prayer out into the quiet.

Tenley's phone rolled to voice mail. Right. She was at the hospital and probably ignoring her phone.

How was he going to pull a rodeo together—one that he didn't even want to take place—in a week?

Chapter Ten

Brody tacked up another flyer on the library's billboard first thing Thursday morning. "Thanks, Miss Williams."

"Tell your sister I'm excited to see her boy ride." The older woman hobbled from behind the counter. Her cane thumped the floor.

"I'll tell her. I've never seen a kid more excited for a rodeo." Brody forced out a smile that felt as plastic as the feed buckets he used. His own enthusiasm waned with every passing day. Three days since he and Callie had argued. She'd left with no word on when she'd return, or if she'd be back in time to help him plan the rodeo. That was her job. Yet, here he stood, tacking up flyers.

He'd typed out a hundred texts but deleted them all before hitting Send.

Luke will be heartbroken. And I'll just be...broken.

"I suppose Tenley won't be reading here this Saturday." Miss Williams eyed the yellow sheet of paper that listed upcoming events. She tapped her cane on the corkboard. "Good thing you're doing. Finally letting the town help out your parents." Her gaze landed on Brody. "I seem to remember trying to set up a meal train a few years ago. Soon after your father's accident."

Brody scuffed the back of his neck. He'd left his hat in the truck out of respect. He missed the opportunity it gave him to hide from this woman's penetrating gaze.

"You told us that it wasn't needed." She huffed and poked her cane into his arm. "I thought you quite foolish at the time." Wrinkles creased her eyes and she let out a barking laugh. "Glad to see you're not as stubborn now. We're good people, Brody. Tamarack Springs loves a chance to come together and show how much we care about each other."

He'd denied them that, out of his own selfishness. She didn't say it, but he heard the censure hidden behind the grandmotherly visage. Her floral skirt swished when she turned away. "See you at the rodeo."

Moving through the glass door, he left the library behind. Humid air stole his breath and dared him to move faster than a snail over a line of salt. Tamarack Springs unrolled on either side. Shop owners across the street flipped their signs to Open and waved at him as he passed. Three blocks of sidewalk led him to Brewsters.

Patrick heaved open the coffee shop's door and pushed a cup into Brody's hand. "For the drive home. You look like you need it."

"Have you been sitting in there waiting for me to leave just so you could give me a coffee?" Brody sipped. Hot liquid scalded his throat and he coughed.

Patrick chuckled. "Poured it the minute I saw you walk out of the library. Saw you drive into town. Said to myself that I've not seen Brody Jacobs in town, except to stop at the feed store, for well over a year. Thought it was time I reminded you that we're still kicking out here."

"Sorry. Been busy." It's not like he'd become some sort of recluse. Had he?

"That reminds me." Patrick snapped his fingers and pushed back into the coffee shop. He held the door open. "Got a second to come inside?"

Brody checked his watch. He'd relegated most of the day for completing Tenley's to-do list, but the habit of saying no almost overwhelmed him. "Sure."

"I won't keep you." Patrick hurried behind the counter and grabbed a box. He pushed it toward Brody. "Your sister asked for donations. I'll bring more as I drive out for the rodeo, but she needed this before Saturday."

Machine parts clanked and rattled. "What is this?"

"Espresso machine. Going to set it up and sell coffees during the auction." Patrick's grin matched so many that Brody had seen the last few days. The people all around town seemed thrilled at the chance to help his family.

He attempted to juggle the coffee so he could hold the box.

Patrick shook his head. "I'll walk you to your truck." He faced the counter. "Man the counter for me, Barb?"

Barb, a short middle-aged woman, nodded and waved Patrick away.

"I've been dismissed." Patrick laughed and hefted the box. "Lead the way."

They stepped back into the summer air.

"Whew." Patrick rubbed his cheek across his shoulder.

Sweat dripped down Brody's back. He'd given up his morning hours of training for this. Given up a chance to make money to help his family. Despite his reservations, this felt more important.

For a long time, he'd resisted letting anyone into his

life. He wanted to do everything himself. To protect his heart.

No more.

His sisters needed this. It was time he looked past his own need to be viewed as strong and capable.

Brody helped Patrick load the espresso machine while finishing his coffee. He slapped the older man on the back. "Thanks for this. I'll take it straight to Tenley."

"Good man." Patrick backed away and brushed his hands down his green apron. "Come by for coffee again sometime. Maybe don't wait another year." He jogged away, waving and calling out "Good morning" to a dozen people while retreating to his shop.

Brody slid into the truck, cranked the engine and turned the air conditioner on full blast. The list Tenley made for him rested in the passenger seat. He reached for it and ticked off the box marked Flyers. What next? He scanned the page.

He'd already called every person on the second list, the potential sponsors and people who might be interested in riding.

If his calculations were correct, they would have a significant turnout for the rodeo. Ah. That was his next mission. Check in with Daniel Wells.

After that, he'd go train Glow. The sooner Callie came back and took the mare, the better.

Two hours later, he pulled up to Daniel's barn and killed the engine. The man waited for him at the barn doors.

If Brody didn't know better, he'd think the man lived in the barn. He seemed to always be there no matter what time Brody arrived. He dropped to the ground and lifted a hand in greeting. "Here to check on the arena."

Daniel's smile beamed. "Almost ready. Been working on it all week. Why don't you come take a look?"

"Why didn't you call me?" Brody trotted after the man. "I would've come and helped."

"Oh, no need. I had plenty of help," Daniel called back over his shoulder. Spry steps carried him ahead of Brody, down the long aisle and into the covered arena.

Brody skidded to a stop at the sight spread out in front of him. Freshly painted white rails gleamed in the light from windows set high in the walls. Sand covered the floor, and not a grain looked to be out of place.

"Wow." He stuck his thumbs in his belt and whistled. "This place looked great before. But you've gone over the top."

"Does a man good to help others." Daniel tilted his head and surveyed the arena. "Been thinking about you and the job I offered. I apologize if it came off as a pity offer."

"No." His pulse bounced. "It isn't that." Brody forced his thoughts into a cohesive line. He'd been avoiding this all week. Every time he came here, the pull intensified. "Tell me something. When you were my age, what did you want out of life?"

Daniel chuckled, the sound rich as it bounced off the arena walls. "I wanted to be a jockey in the Kentucky Derby." He held up a hand to stop Brody when his mouth opened. "Don't say it. No way a six-foot linebacker is getting on the back of a thoroughbred." He shook his head and grinned so wide it took years off. "My dad tried to tell me. I didn't believe him. I was going to be the tallest jockey in history…" He trailed off and ran a hand down his stomach.

"What happened?" Brody kept his gaze averted as Daniel's jaw worked side to side.

The man seemed to still have a lot of emotion invested in his past.

Daniel's smile returned, though not as bright. "Life happened. Reality happened. No one would hire me to ride. I spent years chasing the racehorses." He chuckled at his own pun and shrugged. "Then I decided that if I couldn't race them, I'd train them." A breath breezed out. "At least then I'd get to ride."

"Did you ever have any winners?" Brody winced the minute the question came out. "Sorry. I didn't mean that the way it sounded."

Daniel shifted his feet in the deep sand. "Had lots of winners. Even had one run and win the derby. 'Course that was twenty years ago."

"When did you switch from racehorses to all this?" Brody held out his hand to encompass the estate. He'd seen horses of every discipline during his visits. There didn't seem to be anything Daniel didn't train.

It was Brody's dream come to life. Only at the wrong barn. Was this what he was meant to do? Could he give up the dream of his own barn to obtain the goal of training world-renowned horses?

"Come with me." Daniel turned and motioned for Brody to follow him. They walked away from the arena. The man hooked a left and led Brody to the enormous red barn sitting square on top of the hill facing Daniel's house.

The space was big enough for the entire Jacobs family to move into and never feel crowded. Box stalls lined either side. Several horses stuck their heads out and nickered when Daniel passed. He stopped in front of a dapple-gray gelding and ran his palm over the horse's neck. "Let's say you're at an auction, looking for brood-mares to improve the quality of your colts, and you run across this guy."

Brody stood back and watched man and horse. The gelding leaned into Daniel's touch. White whiskers quivered as the horse worked his lip against Daniel's shirt buttons. He had a sturdy build and plenty of mus-cle. At fifteen hands, he'd make a great all-around rid-ing horse, depending on his nature. Wide-set eyes spoke of intelligence.

Daniel lifted a hand. "Back up." The gelding took a step back, retreating into the stall. "Step left." Again, the horse followed the direction and moved to the left.

"Impressive." Brody had a sudden urge to run home and begin teaching Glow more word commands.

"He wasn't when I bought him. He was a rail-thin, scared, pitiful beast who didn't trust anyone." Daniel snapped his fingers and the gelding spun in a circle, then hurried forward to lip up a peppermint from Dan-iel's outstretched palm. "He'll do anything I ask now. Took me years to teach him. To learn how to work through his fears and reach that willing spirit."

"Why did you do it?" Brody thought he knew the an-swer based on what he now understood of Daniel Wells, but he needed to hear it from the man's own mouth. His hands grew sweaty and he wiped them down his thighs.

"Because I could." Daniel locked his gaze on the wall behind the gelding. "Because no one else would. They looked at him and saw a hopeless animal. They destined him for the glue factory. All because of what his previous trainers did to him. It wasn't his fault. He didn't come into this life with the intention of being terrified to the point that he was labeled as dangerous."

"Too much trouble for too little profit." Brody breathed in and out slowly, letting the sour words settle in his gut. How often had he thought them when deciding whether to take on a new client? His stomach churned.

Daniel faced Brody. His eyes held more understanding and knowledge than any Brody had ever met. "That day, I stopped training for the money. I started training for the horses." He dipped his hat brim toward the fields. "And the money came to me anyway. God blessed my passion and made it profitable. All I want now is to pass that blessing on to someone else."

Him. Brody realized that Daniel wanted to pass this on to him. The lasso of indecision tightened around his neck. He fought back, not ready to concede. He flung his head side to side, reminding himself of a wild mustang trapped with no hope of escape. "It isn't wrong to work for money." He'd been doing his part to take care of his family. He refused to believe that was wrong.

"Never said it was." Daniel shrugged and used his thumb to tip his hat up. Warm brown eyes surveyed Brody's face.

What did the older man see? He looked at horses and saw their potential. What about humans? Did he have the same perceptiveness there?

Brody took a step back, rubbing a hand down his face.

Daniel's eyes warmed.

Brody shook his head. "Looks like you have everything under control here for the rodeo. Call me or Tenley if you need us to come by and help with anything." His thoughts tumbled and spun out of control. He rushed back to his truck and headed home.

Had he been looking at his career under the wrong light all these years? He'd helped countless horses. Riders too. There were safer horses out there because of the time and effort he put into training.

He'd followed his passion. A dampened version of where he saw himself, sure. But not everything a person hoped to achieve was possible. Setbacks happened. Life changed a person's perspective.

Sacrifices were part of growing up.

Brody tightened his grip on the wheel. Grassy fields dotted with cows rolled past. The occasional oak tree provided deep shade over the road and cast his vision into darkness. Did he even want to be the kind of trainer who flitted around the world?

His stomach dropped like he'd swallowed a boulder. He loved his home. The peace of the familiar landscape and being surrounded by family felt as natural as the sunrise. Did he want to give that up for a title?

Callie tightened Glow's girth and then swung into the saddle. She faced the three barrels and settled her wrists on the saddle horn. Sunset littered the sky, fading the world into muted tones that fit her mood. Blues and grays colored the horizon and blended into the green leaves and weathered barn sitting opposite the round pen.

She'd run to Glow's stall the minute she'd returned from the rodeo. Brody's truck was missing and Tenley's house stood empty.

No way she'd pass up an opportunity this perfect. Peace and quiet with Glow.

Leaving for the rodeo had been a mistake. She and

Maverick had rode well. They hadn't won, but she'd learned a lot about the horse Todd wanted to foist on her.

He'd called Glow's retirement "imminent" during the few short minutes they'd chatted outside the arena. His displeasure at Callie's times was obvious. Her heart wasn't in it without Glow.

Glow stomped a hoof and swished her tail. Her ears pricked forward then back toward Callie. Listening.

Callie sucked in one last gulp of air and pushed all the emotions down. She needed to radiate calmness. Her mare's withers twitched and she shook her mane. Callie had misted Glow down with fly spray before they'd left the barn, which meant Glow's twitching might be the mare showing her nervousness.

"Steady, girl." Callie murmured and patted Glow's neck. The mare shook her head, rattling the bit. "Walk on." Callie clucked her tongue and nudged Glow with both heels.

Glow took one step. Then another. Her ears continued swiveling, and her head lifted. She snorted hard enough to cause her sides to shudder. Callie tightened her grip with her knees and urged the mare on. "We can do this."

She patted Glow's shoulder and then tugged on the rein and used her leg to ask for a turn. Glow responded, her body curving a large bow around the barrel. It wasn't perfect. They were several feet from the barrel, but Callie refused to let that dampen her spirit. They were doing it. Glow trusted Callie to keep her safe.

The mare's tail whirled like a helicopter's blades as she picked up on Callie's excitement. She bobbed her head. Callie released a fraction of the tension on the reins and eased Glow into a trot.

Glow's hooves struck hard, bouncing Callie in the saddle. She gritted her teeth and continued the pattern. Left around the second barrel, straight at the third, then another left. "Go home, Glow."

She tapped the mare's sides with her heels. "Go. Go. Go."

The bouncy trot turned into an even worse lope. Without her eyes to guide her, Glow couldn't tell when her hooves would hit and she compensated by striking down hard, sending Callie rocking forward and then back. There was no rhythm, no easy glide, that Callie could match with her seat and legs.

Glow slowed to a walk the instant Callie sat deep in the saddle and tugged on the reins. The mare blew out a snort that sounded as shaky as Callie felt. Everything changed in a matter of a dozen strides. They'd gone from feeling confident to once again feeling insecure in themselves and each other.

Callie dismounted and threw her arms around Glow's neck. "I'm sorry, girl." Glow nudged Callie's back, pushing her closer.

The mare's deep breaths rang out in bellows. Sweat dampened her sides, despite the easiness of the workout, turning her golden hair a muddied brown. Callie wrapped her hands in the flaxen mane and pressed a kiss to the warm neck. They were not done, but she'd made an error. She'd pushed Glow too fast.

Brody would have never made such a rookie mistake.

A lump formed in her throat. Thank goodness, he'd not seen.

"That could have gone better." His voice stretched out, long and smooth as molasses.

Callie's shoulders tensed. She stroked Glow's mane

and kept her back to Brody. "When did you get back?" She'd been so focused on riding that she'd never heard his truck. Or his steps. How much worse would their ride have gone if she'd known he was standing there watching?

"I could ask you the same thing."

She turned then to look at him. He'd taken off his hat, and twin creases lined his forehead. Those used to mean he was worried about something. She didn't dare believe they were there out of concern for her. "Drove in about an hour ago."

"How was the rodeo?" He sounded interested enough, but he didn't look at her as he asked. His attention locked onto Glow and the lines deepened. He lifted a boot onto the bottom rail and lowered his forearms to the middle, leaving him hunkered over like a sloth in midmotion.

Callie released Glow's neck and lifted one shoulder. "No wins."

"That's too bad." He didn't sound sorry at her loss.

Callie swallowed the bitterness coating her tongue. She'd come too far to let Brody's sour attitude ruin her dreams. One more ride for Glow. One more chance to prove that she was worthy.

"Want to try it again?" Brody slipped between the rails and crossed in front of Glow.

The mare followed his steps, using her ears to find him. She lifted her head and whuffled the air.

"Right here, Glow." Brody's voice turned soothing.

Callie tightened her hands into fists until her nails dug into her palms. They were too short to puncture the skin, but the feeling grounded her to the mission.

Brody had made a deal to train Glow.

She needed to use that to her advantage if she wanted

to have a prayer of racing the mare. Nodding, she swung back into the saddle.

A look she couldn't decipher raced across Brody's face. Too many years stretched between them for her to know what he might be thinking. She could assume all day long, but that helped no one.

"What should we do?" She caught a handful of mane along with the reins.

Glow pranced in place, head bobbing up and down. Excitement tightened Callie's muscles. The mare loved this job. If they could just get her confidence back.

"Walk her around the barrels. Nothing else. Give her the signals, patting her neck before reining, but don't try and speed up. Not yet." Brody retreated to the edge of the pen and planted his boots. He crossed his arms and dipped his head.

Darkness cloaked his face, casting his eyes in shadows, but Callie felt them burning into her back when she turned Glow around. How many times would they do this?

Being here with Brody confused her. It poked holes in her desire to race. The rodeo had worn her out to the point that all she wanted was to stay here forever.

No. Not without giving Glow one last chance. Callie bit her lip until blood welled. She needed the money from the win to buy Glow's shares from Sam. The losses on Maverick only made it more necessary that Glow run again.

Callie shook off the heaviness and focused on Glow. The mare was all that mattered right now.

They walked around the barrels. Callie resisted the urge to hold her breath every time Glow turned. Flashes of their crash raced through her mind. Her heart kicked into overdrive.

Glow plodded on, her steps growing steadier the longer they walked.

"Bring it home, Glow," Brody called out, his voice whispering on the summer breeze.

Beneath Callie, the mare's muscles bunched and rippled. Callie relaxed in the saddle when Brody began humming a soft tune. His lilting melody eased Callie's racing pulse.

They could do this. Faith in things hoped for. Wasn't that how the verse went?

Chapter Eleven

She came back.

After catching Callie riding Glow, Brody had spent the rest of the night and most of the next day berating himself for falling back under her charm. He took out his annoyance on the barn, tackling jobs that he usually avoided. Like cleaning all the tack and putting new sand in the round pen. By Friday afternoon, he was tired and still irritable. He stomped up the steps leading into Mom and Dad's house and rolled his shoulders.

The tight muscles screamed and didn't release their tension. Great. Now he was sore and tired. And cranky. He felt like Luke during his Terrible Twos stage. If it would help to lie down and throw a tantrum, he just might do it.

Tenley darted around him, plopped onto the porch swing and kicked the porch, setting the swing into motion. "That's a look I'm coming to understand means trouble." She patted the swaying seat. "Want to talk about it? Everything still a go for the rodeo?"

He passed her a coffee and ran his hand down his face, knocking his hat askew. The rodeo. He'd almost forgotten while dealing with his Callie drama. "Rodeo is fine. All set for tomorrow. What about the dinner and auction? Need any help for that?"

It was becoming easier to let this go. To let Tenley step up and take on a portion of the responsibility. He'd never expected that from his flighty sister.

"Smooth sailing there too." She rubbed her hands together and stopped the swing. "This is really happening. I knew the town would come together, but I didn't know if I'd have to fight you every step of the way."

How pathetic he'd become. He was so entrenched in the idea that no one else could help that he'd built a blockade between him and his sisters. "Being the oldest is supposed to give me the right to protect you."

"And you did." Tenley looked at him from under her lashes. "Maybe you protected us too much."

"What's that mean?"

"Nothing." She puffed out a breath and leaned into the yellow cushion lining the back of the wooden swing. "I don't want to argue tonight. Let's focus on Dad and the fundraiser. Everything else will work itself out."

His recalcitrant sister had secrets. He'd known that for a long time. What surprised him was that no one seemed to know what they were. Tenley kept her innermost thoughts held tight under that head of brown hair. Must be a Jacobs family trait.

Tenley righted his hat when he fell into the swing, her face twisting into a somber grimace. "What's wrong?"

"Nothing. How's Dad?" No way he'd delve into his heart and display his feelings to Tenley. He loved his sister, but this was out of her wheelhouse.

She blinked and then widened her eyes as they sheened

with unshed tears. "Some pain, but he's stable. Doctors said that he was one of the best patients they'd ever had."

Medicine amazed Brody. One minute his dad was in surgery and then he was home none the worse for wear. The discs in his dad's neck were stable, lowering the chance of full paralysis. He heaved a sigh that allowed all the tension to slide from his muscles. *Thank You, Lord, for all You have given my family.*

Tenley stood and paced to the edge of the porch. She put her hip on the railing and stared across the yard. Her folded arms offered a warning. "Remember when we were kids and we'd race down the driveway as fast as we could go?"

"Yeah." Brody followed her line of sight. Horses. Fences. Barns dotting the hillsides. They'd been carefree back then, no worries holding them down.

"You ever want to do it again? Just toss everything aside and race into the unknown?"

"No." Brody locked his gaze on Tenley's house where Callie stood on the front porch, a silhouette against the afternoon sun. She'd come back from town and gone straight to Tenley's. They were due a discussion, but not right now. He needed to cool his temper first. The last thing he wanted was something else unpredictable cropping up to fuel the pain. "I'm going to see Dad."

He stood and pushed into the house while removing his hat. The smell of bread and roasting vegetables set his stomach to growling worse than a hibernating bear's.

Tenley let him leave. When he glanced back, she stood in the same place, a contemplative expression drawing her mouth into a frown. What was up with his sister?

Brody nodded at Mom and moved down the hallway

to Dad's room. He settled in the black, leather recliner and crossed his ankle over his knee. The fan at Dad's bedside table sent a rush of air to cool the sweat beading on Brody's temples.

Dad grunted. "I'm the one who had surgery, but you're the one who looks like you're in pain."

"You're awake." Brody stated the obvious to divert from what his face revealed. Even post-surgery, his dad had a knack for knowing his kids and working out their problems.

His father's laughter rasped. He winced and gripped the sheets. "How are things at the barn?"

Yet another topic Brody would rather avoid, but he needed advice. "I'm considering training for Daniel Wells." The offer had come weeks ago, but he'd avoided it. After his talk with Daniel yesterday, it refused to go back into the darkness and hide.

He would no longer be his own boss, but the pay would be steady. For the first time, they had a chance to climb out of debt and stare freedom in the eye if the fundraiser didn't do as well as Tenley hoped.

Brody reserved judgment for once the event ended. *Never depend on one event to cover a lifetime of debt.* Though, wasn't that exactly what had happened when Jesus died on the cross? He ruffled a hand through his hair. Great. Now he was getting philosophical. Or was it theological? This was why he worked with horses. Easier than playing brain games all day.

"Daniel Wells." Dad raised his eyes to the ceiling. "Good man. Great trainer. How do you feel about that?"

"Shocked." Brody leaned back and clasped his hands behind his head. "This could be the answer to our prayers."

"That so?" Amusement lit Dad's voice. His rasping laugh turned into a cough. "Didn't know you were privy to my prayers."

"You don't want to pay off the bills?"

"Life is about more than getting out of financial debt. Would that I knew that sooner." He speared Brody with a look that could melt plastic. "You need to stop trying to take care of everyone else and focus on yourself or you're going to wake up one day and realize you missed out."

Missed out? He'd already lost out on a life with Callie, and she was about to leave for the last time. While he stayed here, where he belonged. It's how things were meant to be. One thing he'd learned from talking to Daniel, Brody no longer sought the fame of being a world-traveling trainer. The work he did here was enough. It satisfied him. The only thing he regretted was not getting the debt paid sooner so that Tenley didn't feel the need to take it on for herself.

"You still determined to give up your dreams and stagnate here?" Dad huffed.

"What do you mean?" He'd done the only thing possible. Dreams changed. He had all he needed. Maybe he still hoped to do something great in the upcoming years, after his family was taken care of.

"Stop thinking so much." Dad gripped Brody's hand. "You spent ten years taking care of us, even when we told you to go."

"You needed me here." It was the monster in the room. The words he'd lived by. The ones he whispered every time a chance to leave cropped up. His family needed him. Callie had walked away and lived her dreams without him. She'd never needed him. Not even when they were kids.

Dad's sigh gusted. "You were comfortable here. The

last thing a parent wants is to see their child in pain. You hid yours so well, I think we let ourselves believe you were happy, but that isn't true anymore. The longer Callie stays, the more I see that gleam in your eye. Dreams change, but they don't always go away after being denied. So, I'll ask you, and I want you to answer truthfully. Where do you want to be in ten more years?"

Brody started to answer that he was happy right here, but Dad squeezed again, and the pain of pinched fingers forced his mouth shut.

Where did he want to be? Ten years felt like forever, but he knew it would pass in a blink. Before Callie left, he'd imagined them right back here once she got as many buckles as she could win and he'd trained a horse from nothing to famous.

Mom knocked on the door. "Brody, the farrier is here."

He nodded. "See you later, Dad." He had to get away. His mind couldn't keep up with the impending threat that might topple his carefully laid tower. If he wasn't needed here, then who was he? What was the goal of his life if not to care for his parents?

"Think about what I said." Dad's gaze followed Brody as he left. His words followed far longer.

Lily was already out of her truck and moving her tools to the ground outside the front of the barn. "Hey, Brody. Who's first?"

"Grace and then Glow."

Lily's head snapped up. She gripped the handle of her rasp, hands twisting. "Glow? As in, Callie Wade's Golden Glow?" Exultation crossed her face. "I heard she was in town, but to get to put shoes on a horse like that? It's a farrier's dream. Is she running soon? Am I going to get to say that the shoes I put on Golden Glow actually touched a championship arena?"

"Maybe." Brody let Lily's joy fill the air. Her excitement settled him.

Callie jogged down from Tenley's house, her ponytail flapping. "Hey, Lily. How's your dad?"

"Great. Enjoying retirement, though he still tries to tell me about every horse in the county. Did you know that the O'Malleys' mare is eighteen years old and has foundered twice? Has to have corrective shoes every spring."

"I had no idea." Callie slapped her hands together. "Can I help?"

Lily looked for Brody to answer. When he didn't, she nodded at Callie. "Sure. What are you doing, Brody?"

What was he doing? Brody walked away without answering. Answers were as scarce as horses on the moon.

Callie helped Lily carry her tool kit into the barn before going to retrieve Grace. The mare bopped her head up and down on every stride. Excitement caused the mare's muscles to twitch, and her nose lifted into the air. "You're going to behave today." Callie said it firmly, infusing her voice with determination.

Lily's eyebrows scrunched when she saw the mare. She nodded at Callie. "You can tie her to the barn there." She pointed her rasp at an eyebolt twisted into the barn wall.

At the other end of the barn, Brody banged around the stalls. Manure sailed out and landed in the wheelbarrow.

Callie tightened her hands on the lead rope. "Do you mind if I try holding her? Brody gave me permission to train her."

Lily upraised a shoulder. "I don't mind. Try and keep her away from my tools. Last time, she chucked her horseshoes into another stall."

"I'll do my best." Callie smiled, the move feeling tight across her cheeks.

Grace tossed her head. Callie stroked the long neck and shushed the mare. She risked a quick glance toward the stall where Brody worked. What was bothering him today? He seemed determined to avoid her whenever possible. Probably because she'd ridden Glow without him yesterday.

But Glow belonged to her…as far as he knew. It was her right to ride the mare.

"Okay, girl. Let's go." Lily slid her hand down the mare's leg and lifted the hoof.

Callie focused on the horse, dragging her attention away from Brody. He sauntered out of the stall, his profile appearing in her peripheral vision. One hand lifted to wipe his forehead. If this was her paying attention, then she had a long way to go.

"How do you like being a farrier?" She scratched Grace's head when the mare started inching her nose toward the toolbox.

Lily spoke while bent at the waist and picked out the horse's hooves. "Been my dream for as long as I remember. Dad didn't want me to do it. Too hard on the body. Too dangerous." She dropped the hoof and patted Grace's side. "But I tell you what, these horses make it worth it. The good ones, especially."

"I'm hoping to turn her into a good one." Callie needed this win. After the failed rides on Glow, anything that helped boost her confidence came as a bonus.

Lily's laughter rang through the barn. "This isn't

bad. I have stories that could lift the hair off your head."
She returned to her work, leaving Callie too much time
to think.

Grace lipped Callie's shirt, her soft muzzle wiggling
side to side. Her ears pricked straight forward, but she
didn't try to pull away from Lily. The little jumper appeared steady as a rock. Curious but steady.

"I'd like to see what you can do over the hurdles."
Callie ran her palm over the mare's ears.

Lily moved on to another hoof. "She's pretty as a
picture. Perfect form. Sails right over anything you put
in front of her."

"I almost wish I'd learned more than Western riding."
Callie released a huff of laughter. "Not like I'd have time
for more than one discipline."

"No rule that says you have to stick to just one thing."

True. But when she took time into consideration,
there simply were not enough hours in the day to take
on more responsibilities. Glow had to be her priority.

Lily finished Grace's hooves and straightened. She
planted her hands on her lower back and stretched. "Dad
had one thing right. This job will do a number on the
bones and muscles."

A flash of red shot down the aisle. Callie swiveled
in time to see Luke barrel to Ranger's stall and climb
onto the door. He stopped with his arms hanging over
the edge. Seconds later, Molly and Brody converged at
the stall door. Ranger nudged Luke's outstretched hand
and the boy giggled. "We're racing tomorrow, Ranger."
Luke glanced at Brody and frowned. "You're doing the
relay with me, right?"

Brody nodded. His lips flattened into a thin line.

Callie tipped her head in their direction. Brody was going to ride in the rodeo?

"Do you need to practice?" Brody plucked Luke from the door and settled him on the ground.

He nodded so fast, his little Stetson flopped over his eyes. "We need lots of practice." He swiveled on his heels and called down the hall, "Can you teach me some more?" The hopefulness pinched her heart.

She'd neglected helping Luke after his birthday. Everything except her determination to ride Glow in another rodeo had been cast to the side. Would she ever stop thinking about no one other than herself?

Luke, Brody and Molly headed out the far end of the barn with Ranger in tow. The paint clip-clopped down the aisle, his nose brushing the top of Luke's hat. Callie knew horses well enough to understand that the gelding already loved Luke. Their bond had been as instant as Callie's with Glow.

Grace nudged her head against Callie and she returned to stroking the mare. "You're almost done."

"Last one." Lily raised the left front hoof and set it on the stand where she could run the rasp without practically standing on her head. The female farrier completed the job in minutes. With one last rasp, she dropped the hoof back to the ground and patted Grace's shoulder. "Atta girl." She brushed her hands down her half chaps and grinned. "Now, let's see Glow. I've waited all my life for a chance like this."

Callie swallowed her immediate reaction as fear bubbled up. Did she tell Lily about Glow's blindness? What if she didn't and Glow got scared at the sounds? Callie's heart slammed against her ribs in double time. She led Grace to her stall and retrieved Glow. "You can do this."

"Wow." Lily leaned on a doorframe and whistled as Glow approached. "She looks even better in person."

The lump in Callie's throat grew too big to ignore. She ran her hands over Glow's ears and puffed up her cheeks. "Lily, I need to tell you something, but I need you to keep it a secret." Her tone came out gritty, the need evident in her clipped words.

Lily pushed her hands through her hair and straightened her ponytail. "Whatever you need, Callie."

"Glow's blind. This is the first time she's had shoes put on since it happened." Her voice quivered, and it took all her effort to keep tears from trickling down her cheeks. It was all becoming too real. What she was attempting to do, running a blind horse at full speed and making hairpin turns, it sounded impossible.

The farrier blinked, her mouth open in an O. She walked all the way around Glow once Callie stopped the mare. She ran a hand down Glow's front leg but didn't ask for her to raise her hoof. "Have you been picking out her feet like usual?"

"Yes." Callie nodded and brushed strands of hair from her sticky forehead. She'd left her hat at the house in her rush to get to the barn.

Lily went all the way around Glow again, rubbing each leg. "How does she react?"

"Stands still and quiet. Same as always."

"We'll start slow." Lily reached for her hoof pick and squared her shoulders. She walked to Glow's head and leaned in close to Glow's ears. "We're going to be fine, aren't we, pretty girl." Confidence oozed from her. She looked up at Callie. "This will be a first for us both. Never shod a blind horse. First time for everything."

Callie kept up her gentle patting and encouragement.

Lily started at Glow's shoulder and ran her hand down the right front leg. She tugged, asking Glow to lift. The horse shifted her weight and raised the hoof.

"Half the battle done." Sweat dripped from Lily's brow as she went to work.

Other than a twitch every now and then, Glow remained frozen, only moving when Lily asked something of her.

Callie let out a gusty breath when the last hoof hit the ground.

Lily wiped a damp towel over her face and beamed a smile. "That does it." She patted Glow's flank. "She's a winner. You've known that for years, but this is just beyond me. Never knew a blind horse could be this easygoing."

If only that same easy energy followed her when Callie sat in the saddle. They needed explosive energy and calm detachment from the panic that drove them both faster and faster.

How did she get that back? Did Glow even have one last run in those long, golden legs?

Chapter Twelve

Rodeo day dawned crisp and bright. Callie breathed it in. Popcorn. Cheers from the crowd in the stands. Excitement tinged the air, giving it an electric hum that traveled down Callie's spine. It might be just a fundraiser rodeo for the Jacobses, but it made her happy. More than happy.

Callie stood aside as Brody rode past on a pinto gelding. He'd acquired the horse from a couple who were moving and couldn't take the animal along. At a little over fifteen hands, the horse would be a perfect starting mount for a younger rider. Brody hadn't named the pinto yet. She thought she knew why, but she kept her thoughts to herself.

Luke trailed behind on Ranger, his grin the thing of dreams as the little boy gripped his horse's mane and waved at Molly across the arena.

"You've done it, Tenley." Callie faced the woman at her side and offered a quick hug.

Tenley dashed at her eyes and peered around the ring. Daniel Wells had come through in a big way, giving Tenley access to the barns and arenas for the fundraiser. All without charging them a dime. Tenley appeared to be over the moon with excitement as she danced on her toes. "Are you coming to the dance later? We've decorated the big barn with lights and there's going to be food. Molly baked a cake."

Callie's stomach rumbled at the mention of food and Tenley grinned.

"I'll think about it." She'd appear for Peter and Margaret.

"And don't forget the auction. Mr. Wells is offering a mare for people to bid on. One of his best mares." Tenley crossed her arms over the top rail and squinted her eyes at Brody as he raced past with the flag billowing in the wind. "I tried to get Brody to bid on her but he thinks it'd be in poor taste for the family to bid on items during a fundraiser like this."

"He's probably right." Callie swallowed the lump in her throat. He'd been right about so many things. Her breath caught and she stepped back from the arena. "I'm going to check on the horses."

There was nothing to do. Not really, but she needed away from here. Away from this family that made her want to stay when her life was outside Tamarack Springs. She'd always thought she'd come back, maybe take a trip through town just to satisfy the urge to plant roots and then race off for the next rodeo. Spending time with Brody made those dreams of growing old together dig in and root out everything else.

She wanted to stay, and it was his turn to fly. With the bills paid through this fundraiser, Brody would have a chance to snatch the dream he'd left behind. She refused to be the thing standing in his way.

Callie hurried off, boots clopping as her steps picked up until she was running. She spun into the barn and darted inside the office. A brand-new saddle rested on a red stand, ready for auction. Callie had talked the woman from the photo shoot in Kentucky into donating for the fundraiser.

The poster behind the saddle showed a large-as-life Callie. She smiled from the saddle, her hair windswept and her clothes perfectly pressed. It was what her sponsors had wanted to see. A mirage used to entice riders to the rodeo. That wasn't the real Callie. She was cowboy hats and braids down the middle of her back. Dirt on her hands and mud on her boots. Combing Glow as they prepared for a race and spending the night in the barn as anxious nerves refused to let her sleep.

Tamarack Springs knew the real Callie Wade. The rodeo knew this…imposter.

"You're about to miss Luke's first solo run." Brody moved up beside her, his broad shoulders filling the doorway.

Patrick sat behind the table set up next to her poster, passing out tickets to a line of people. He'd closed the coffee shop to come here and help out. Most of the town had shut down today and sat in the stands or on the backs of horses.

Tears burned at the devotion of her hometown. There was no place in the world like this. Someday she'd come back again, maybe for good.

"You'd better get ready for the relay." Molly rushed up and grabbed each of them by the sleeve. "Luke's counting on you to be waiting for him."

Callie backed out of the office and placed a palm over her racing heart. Luke. The little boy stole her heart with a single smile, much like his uncle all those years ago.

Her phone burned in her pocket, the missive from Todd clear as daylight in the text he'd sent. She was due at the barn. No more excuses. They'd watch Glow run and then make their decision. Callie knew what that decision would be. Glow wasn't ready. They still didn't know about the blindness.

"You okay?" Concern etched Brody's brow. He took her hand in his, his thumb trailing across her knuckles. A single touch from Brody should not be enough to make her want to change everything about her future. But it did. It had ten years ago and she'd bolted out of fear that if she didn't leave, she'd never get away.

Would a life here with Brody have been that bad?

Callie shook her head, tossing away her reminiscing and focusing on the arena where Luke sat in Ranger's saddle and twisted to look over his tiny shoulder. Luke chewed on his lip and knotted his fingers in Ranger's mane. Teaching Luke had been one of the highlights of coming home.

Home.

She missed it. Missed them.

"I want you to come with me."

Brody frowned and his hand tightened on hers. "Where?"

"When I leave for the rodeo. Come and help me with Glow."

His breath hitched. "Callie, I can't leave."

"Why not? Your father's medical bills will be paid up, if the ticket sales are any indication. You're not obligated to stay now. You can pursue your dreams."

"What if my dreams have changed? What if my dreams are right here, with you? A life on the ranch." He pulled her across the aisle, his touch gentle despite his strength. "I can do great things without spending all my time traveling away from home. I'm happy here. Maybe you can be happy here too."

Could she? An urge to stay by his side turned her bones soft. Callie leaned into him and put an arm around his waist. She could see them working together, day after day, until they grew too old and had to turn the training over to their kids. Would they have kids? They'd never talked about it.

Brody deserved to be a dad. He'd be a great father. What about her? Would she be a good mother? Her own mother couldn't stand motherhood and had been more than happy to pawn Callie off on the Jacobses.

Would she be the same? Would the call of the rodeo be too much to walk away from?

"I need to do this. My contract says I have to ride."

"Glow isn't ready."

"Then they'll put me on another horse. But I need to try." She moved to face him and put her palms to his cheeks. Callie tugged and he lowered his face to hers. His breath whispered over her cheek, the rim of his hat bumping hers. "Come with me. Just one time. I want to ride my last rodeo with you by my side. Let me accomplish that dream before I move on."

"Last rodeo?" Brody's pulse jumped in his neck, the rapid beat pounding under her thumb. "You're leaving the rodeo?"

"I'm tired, Brody. Tired of chasing the rodeo from state to state. Tired of living out of my truck and never knowing whether I'll make enough money to ever stop depending on my sponsors. My contract ends after this rodeo, and I don't plan on renewing. Come with me and help me say goodbye." She couldn't say why she needed him there, only that it felt right to show Brody the life she was giving up. One show with him standing beside her. She'd ridden alone for ten years, and she wanted this one to be different.

"What if you get there and you change your mind?" His voice dropped, the tone rich and warm in the summer air. A hint of breeze stirred the leaves on the oaks lining the drive. Horses stamped their hooves and the crowd shouted as the rider before Luke trotted from the arena.

The tag-team runs completed with the boy's exit. The crowd roared their approval.

"Up next, single barrel relay race." An older man Callie didn't recognize stood on a short platform on the far side of the arena. He lifted his hands over his head and waved. "Up first, we have Luke, Kaitlyn and Bryce." The three younger riders lined up at the starting line.

Callie took Brody's shoulders and planted a kiss on his cheek. "We'll talk about it later. Luke needs us right now."

A group ran out into the arena and set up the single barrel at the end of the track. The goal was to run to the end, circle the barrel, then race back. Once the rider crossed the line, the second rider in the relay repeated the pattern. First team to get all three members back across the line won.

"We better mount up." Callie scooted away from Brody and rushed to her horse. She'd tested Spirit on the run yesterday and he loved the barrels. He stood tied to the hitching post outside the barn. A dozen kids surrounded him, all of them in awe of his resemblance to the horse from the movies.

They squealed and clapped when Callie swung into the saddle. "Let's go, big guy." He responded to her every shift in weight and they lined up behind Brody on the paint. The three geldings jangled their bits and arched their necks.

A bicycle horn beeped, courtesy of the announcer. Luke and Ranger shot down the track. Luke held on tight and wheeled the gelding around the barrel. Ranger stretched out, legs pumping as he threw clumps of sand in his wake. Everyone cheered them on.

Callie gave Luke a high five after he dismounted. "Way to go. That's what I call a perfect run."

"Do you think we'll win?"

Oh, man. She was not equipped to answer this question right now. Her heart told her to say that having fun was all that mattered. But the truth was that she wanted to win. That drive of competition kept her going long after the fun wore off.

Brody thundered their way. Sand sprayed as he pulled the gelding into a sliding stop.

Callie gathered up her reins and nudged Spirit into a run. The gelding took off. Every stride rekindled her love for this, the adrenaline, the feel of a horse doing its best just for her. The cheers didn't hurt either. They spun around the barrel and Callie whooped.

She had no idea who was winning. For the first time in her life, she hadn't sized up the competition. She ran for the love of it.

Luke pumped his fist in the air as they flashed past. "We did it."

Breathing hard, Callie leaped to the ground, pulled Luke from his saddle and spun him around in a circle. "Your first rodeo win."

"I hope it doesn't make him want to compete professionally." Molly rushed over and hugged Luke and Callie at the same time.

Callie reeled back from the words. They struck her in the heart, splitting her in two.

"Callie." Molly's voice rose and she used her hand to cover her mouth. "I didn't mean it like that."

Luke glanced between them and then pulled himself back into Ranger's saddle. "Can we take Ranger to the barn? I want to show him all the other horses."

Molly swallowed hard and gripped Callie's arm. "Please, believe me. I was joking with you." Her expression radiated concern and regret. "I would never hold him back from his dreams. If rodeo is his future, then that's where he'll go." She took a breath. "Just not yet."

And Callie was not supposed to encourage him. Noted. She took Spirit's reins and mounted, then urged the horse in the opposite direction. "It's okay, Molly. I'll be gone soon, and he'll probably forget all about the rodeo in a few years. Most kids go through a phase."

"Callie." Molly's tone begged for Callie to turn around. She couldn't. If she met Molly's gaze, she'd fall apart.

Brody rode alongside and slowed the gelding to match Spirit's pace. "Was that necessary?"

Not at all.

Brody reached over and put his hand on her shoulder. They stopped on the track between two barns. People milled around, most of them carrying plates of food. New scents tantalized on each breath. Smoked chicken sent curls of aroma into the air from the smokers tucked behind one of Daniel's barns.

Their previous conversations stacked onto this one, creating a tottering tower that threatened to fall at any moment. It was too much. Caring about Brody and the others hurt when it came time to leave. She'd failed to guard her heart against them.

"Callie, I want you to stay." The words seemed to wrench themselves from Brody.

Air caught in her lungs and cinched her throat closed. They were right back where they'd started ten years ago. She wanted to stay, same as before.

"I can't explain why I have this insatiable need for one more run." She crossed her wrists over the saddle horn. The horses walked toward the nearest barn, where their trailers were parked outside. Her pulse jumped and banged so hard, she felt off balance. "I'm leaving the rodeo, Brody. And when I do, I need to find a new way to live my life. I can't do that until I finish what I started. This run, Glow's last run, is what I need to feel like we gave it our best effort. I can't—I won't—let us go out with that crash as our last ride."

The passion in her words filled her and steadied her, pulling her breathing back to normal.

"You know what you're facing." Brody made it a statement.

Callie tucked her chin. The challenges waiting for her and Glow were skyscraper high but not impossible to leap. They just had to have faith and trust. A blind horse and a rider who refused to give up.

The call for the barrel racers to begin mounting up jolted Callie. "We should get the horses put away. Luke will be expecting us to watch."

Brody didn't answer, merely walked into the barn and began untacking his horse.

Callie followed and tossed her tack in her trailer. She wouldn't be riding again tonight. They hurried to their seats, settling in beside Margaret and Molly as the women cheered for Luke. They were on the bottom bleacher, where Peter could sit in his wheelchair and be comfortable in the shade.

Brody's questions warred with her newfound determination. Would she change her mind? Would the rush of adrenaline that came from galloping hooves prove too much to overcome?

"Luke, take your place." The announcer waved toward the gate.

Luke dipped his head at the announcer and leaned forward in the saddle. Ranger broke into an easy trot and carried Luke safely around the three barrels. All the kids in this division were ages five and under, all new to barrel racing and with orders to keep their mounts to nothing faster than a trot. Luke had tried to argue at first, stating that he and Ranger knew how to lope and could blow the competition away if they were given the chance.

Callie had finally gotten through to Luke when she'd reminded him that not every challenge was meant to end with an all-out race to the finish. Sometimes, a person had to take things slow. Evaluate the path in front of them and decide if it was safe.

She eyed Brody from the side. And sometimes the path before you was so littered with the past that it looked impassable. But God knew how to make a way. She ran her hand over her eyes and cheered as Luke crossed the finish line with the best time so far. Only two more kids to run and they'd announce the winner.

God, are You showing me the way?

Brody followed the line of trucks back home. They shut off engines simultaneously and doors began slamming shut. Luke had won the barrel racing competition and couldn't stop talking about the rodeo.

He rubbed a hand over his face and let out a sigh. They didn't have a final number yet, but based on what Tenley was told, Dad's medical bills might be completely paid for. The weight of ten years lifted from his shoulders all at once. Was this it?

The rodeo at the Wells Riding Academy had gone over with a bang. The kids had loved it. The parents had had a great time. He'd almost lost it when he'd seen the auction. Every person in Tamarack Springs must have been there. Bids flew faster than robins' chatter. The horse had sold for a ridiculous amount to Mr. and Mrs. Simmons. They'd then approached Callie and asked if she'd ever consider giving riding lessons. She'd appeared shocked.

Brody didn't blame her.

Her words came back and lingered. She wanted to leave the rodeo. And do what? They'd not reached that part of the conversation. Only that she wanted him to go with her and watch her last ride.

He didn't know if he could.

That part of Callie's life felt so separate from life here at the ranch. For him to venture into that world risked tearing the scab off the wound that finally felt healed and exposing it to the world.

What if he went and found out that he was the one now enamored with the rodeo life? He couldn't leave his family and follow Callie to the rodeo. It was a ridiculous notion.

"If you think any harder, your brain is going to run away screaming." Tenley nudged him with an arm and waved toward the barn. "What's up with you two today?

I expected you to be happy. This is the answer we've needed for ten years and you haven't even said thank you."

Right. He was a terrible brother. Brody gripped the back of his neck and lifted his face to the moonlight. Stars stared back from the heavenly canopy. Frogs bellowed from the pond, their voices resonating into the night. "Thank you for doing this, Tenley." He hugged her close and then stole her hat, tossing it to Molly, who stood with her back leaned on her truck's hood.

Molly caught the hat and spun it around on her finger. "Is this the big secret you've been keeping from all of us, or is there something else hiding in that brilliant brain of yours?"

Tenley's guilty look had Brody's heart racing.

"What's wrong?"

"Nothing." Tenley pulled free and rolled her shoulders. She winced, no doubt feeling the same weight that had bogged him down.

He'd wanted to spare his sisters from that, but it seemed that, no matter what he did, his sisters were there to take on responsibility no family should encounter.

"Come on, Ten. What's up?"

She huffed and snatched her hat back from Molly. She slammed it onto her head and folded her arms while scowling. "There's nothing to talk about. Yet." She stomped away, leaving Molly and Brody behind.

Brody watched her go, tempted to chase her down and demand to know why she refused to talk to them. Stubbornness was a Jacobs family trait. One that had brought them through many hard times. He regretted it now.

Molly shook her head. "Don't, Brody."

"What if she's struggling and won't tell us?"

"Then we turn it over to God. That's all we can do. You can't make Tenley do what you want."

Turn it over to God. Why did he always have trouble doing that?

Chapter Thirteen

Sunday had passed in the slow cadence of church and peaceful reminiscing. Brody had refused to do anything more arduous than kick off his boots and reach for a magazine.

But now it was Monday. A new day. A new week. A thousand new chances to help Callie get Glow running. He'd tried to back away and let them go.

They were anchored in his heart. Every beat sang a song for Callie.

He made his way to the barn, coffee cup in one hand and a list of chores in the other. Time ticked down to Callie's last day. They were cutting it close. Glow still ran choppy on the lope and cut wide on the turns.

A truck rumbled up the drive, another sleek rig not unlike Callie's. Sunlight caught on the silver and chrome and flashed into Brody's eyes. He lowered his hat and moved to intercept the driver.

Samantha Blade dropped to the ground in front of him and gave a saucy smile. "Well, well. I think I see now what brought Callie home."

What was Callie's partner doing here? "Can I help

you, Miss Blade?" Uncertain of their standing, he opted for friendliness.

"Oh, call me Sam." She nudged him with her elbow. "Everybody does."

"Right." Brody waited a beat but, when no answer came, he tried again. "What are you doing here?" Well now, that had come out harsher than he'd intended, but Brody bit back his apology. If this woman was here to drag Callie back to the rodeo before she and Glow were ready, Sam would have to go through him first.

"I came to check on my horse." She tipped her head to the sky and spun on her heel. "Quite a place you have here. Callie told me about you. How good you are with the horses. Ever thought about training rodeo horses?"

So Sam didn't know everything. Or she did and she was using this as an excuse to ferret out information. She leaned to the side.

Brody locked his posture, blocking Sam from seeing into the barn. "I'm afraid I don't know what you're talking about. I don't have any of your horses here."

Her eyes narrowed, her spine straightening and hands going to her hips. "Oh, but you do. Golden Glow. How's she doing? The vet plans to drop by this afternoon for a soundness check since Callie couldn't provide any information for Todd during her last ride. I wanted to see her for myself. I'm on my way to the next rodeo and decided to swing by."

He staggered back at her words, disbelief sending shockwaves down his arms. Not possible. Callie would never sell Glow. He opened his mouth to say so when a glint in Sam's eyes halted the flood of words.

"Sam?" Callie's voice emerged from the barn. Her steps hit the ground, moving fast.

Brody had his back to Callie, but her voice sounded full of fear. Her steps skipped across the drive, gravel crunching under her boots. She came to a stop beside Brody. "What are you doing here? I thought you were in Texas."

Sam scoffed. "I've not been in Texas for a week. Big rodeo in South Carolina this weekend. I loaded up Sweetheart and headed over after we spoke Saturday. Thought we'd spend some time catching up. How's Glow?"

"Fine." Callie's answer came too quick, her breath leaving in a rush. Her eyes darted to Brody then slid away.

He knew then that Callie had secrets beyond his imagining. Fury sparked. He'd trusted her. For however brief a time. He'd thought the Callie of his childhood, the girl she was before she'd left them, had returned. Now he knew better. He faced her and Callie paled as he spoke. "You don't own Glow." His words were razor-sharp, no question allowed to permeate the statement.

He'd known something about the situation hadn't added up, but he'd put it off as a result of the accident and Glow's blindness.

"I can explain." Callie moved closer and gripped his arm. Ice-cold fingers dug into his skin and begged him to stand by her side.

He considered throwing off her hand, but the glint in Sam's eyes never wavered. She was enjoying this, enjoying tormenting Callie, and he'd have no part in anything that hurt her. Swallowing his pride and the burn of deceit, he waited.

Callie swallowed and licked her lips. "I didn't do well those first years in the rodeo." She grimaced and her grip flexed. "I almost came back about three years in, with nothing to show for my trouble. Sam offered me a way out. She'd had a good run and the sponsors were begging her to sign on. She offered to buy seventy percent of Glow's ownership to keep me going. It was that or come crawling back here as a failure."

And Callie Wade didn't know how to fail. She'd clawed her way into the rodeo without any help from her semi-famous parents, and he knew—deep in his heart, he knew—that she'd never quit until she had no other choice. She had something to prove, and something as insignificant as a lack of funds would not stand in her way.

He could almost understand. What wouldn't he have done to change his own fate back then?

Brody realized the truth behind the pain clutching at him. He wasn't upset that Callie had sold Glow. The horse was hers to do whatever she willed, even if he'd spent most of his teenage years helping her train Glow to be a champion. What hurt was the fact that she'd not trusted him with the truth when she'd arrived.

"Why didn't you tell me?" He needed that question answered. Above all else, he needed to hear her reasoning. Maybe then he could learn a way to put it behind him and move on.

Callie rubbed her forehead. "Because I was afraid you wouldn't help me." She looked up and her eyes filled. "I don't have the money to buy Glow back from Sam. Not until I win another race."

Disappointment wrapped around his stomach, clenching it tight. The rest of her words sank in. She didn't trust him. And she'd lied to him. He tipped his hat back and scratched at his head. A thousand words ran through his mind. He kept them all corralled. Anything he had to say, he'd say it when Samantha Blade wasn't watching like they were the best new drama show.

* * *

It was all going wrong. Callie took a moment to breathe and looked Sam in the eye. What was the woman doing here? There had to be more to it than a simple passing through to check on Glow. Sam had never cared what Callie did, so long as they continued to compete.

It almost defied reason that Sam had helped Callie out way back when. A competitor buying her opponent's horse and letting her continue to ride said horse? Unheard of.

So why? Callie had never bothered to ask before out of fear, but now that her secret was out in the open, Callie saw no reason not to let loose. "What would it cost me to buy Glow back from you?" She knew what she'd paid. Knew what Glow was worth as a 1D barrel racer, but what side angle would Sam play?

Sam crossed her arms and cocked her head. Callie recognized the mischief in her eyes. Sam named a figure well out of Callie's price range, almost double the mare's actual worth. It had been a mistake to mention her money woes in front of Sam.

Brody's eyes narrowed and he took a stance that Callie recognized. He was preparing to go into battle. For her and Glow. After everything she'd done, all the half-truths and trouble she'd brought to his door, and the ripping out of his heart, he still moved to confront the blockade halting her path.

Callie paused then released a weighted breath in a rush. *Please, Lord. Give me strength.* She moved in front of Brody and confronted Sam. Time to end the charade. "Glow's blind, Sam."

Her friend barked out a harsh laugh and rocked on her bootheels. "Nice try, Callie." She stopped when Callie didn't move and her hands fell to her sides. "You're serious? Blind...but how—"

"Does it really matter?" Brody interrupted before Callie launched into the logistics of Glow's disease. "Does it affect your selling price?"

Sam pursed her lips, her expression calculating. "What's stopping me from taking her to auction right now?"

"The fact that you'll get pennies for her. Not the price you just gave me, obviously. You're using her sentimental value against me when you know I can't afford to pay that much."

"Exactly." Sam shrugged a shoulder. "It's all about business, Callie. I want a return on my investment."

"You won't get one unless you're willing to negotiate. Take her to auction, if you want. We'll just follow you and buy her ourselves." Brody anchored himself by Callie's side, and she felt the heat emanating from his skin where his arm brushed hers. "Take her, if you want. Sounds like we'll get the better deal."

Callie entreated Sam with a look. "Come on, Sam. Don't be cruel. What if it was Sweetheart or Rocket? Put yourself in my shoes and tell me what you'd want me to say if our roles were reversed."

"I'd say you have an obligation to tell your sponsors that you don't have a horse to ride." Sam turned on her heel. "If you don't call them, I will." She strode away. "I'll let you know what I decide about Glow."

Callie faced Brody, her body tight as adrenaline coursed through her veins. A breeze tickled the hairs on the back of her neck. "I'll be back soon." She ran after Sam and climbed into the truck's cab before Sam could put the truck in gear and pull away.

"What are you doing?" Sam narrowed her eyes.

"Talking." She waved her hand at the barn. "Let's go into town, grab some coffee and talk this over. I'll call my sponsors while we're there. You can hear the whole conversation." Her heart ached. One day of success followed by the barrel of defeat. No doubt her sponsorship was about to end. Sam knew about Glow and soon so would the entire world.

They were out of time. Out of resources.

Brody spun on his heel and marched for the barn.

Sam wheeled them toward town, her gaze locked on the road.

"How was Texas?" Callie cleared her throat.

Sam shook her head. "Not right now. Give me a chance to think. Once we're at the coffee shop and I have an espresso in my hand, we'll talk this through."

Callie let the rudeness slide. Sam usually didn't mean anything by her direct approach, she went through life the same way she rode. To the point. No wasted energy and nothing given without something in return. Callie used the free time to contemplate what she might offer Sam to sweeten her into letting Glow go at a price Callie could afford.

Once they were sitting at the coffee shop, Callie pulled her phone from her pocket and dialed. Todd answered on the second ring and Callie let the words fall between them, slicing through her future as cleanly as a knife through butter. "Golden Glow is blind. I don't know if she'll be ready to run in the stampede."

Chatter built around Callie as Todd remained silent. Customers drifted through the door and placed their orders. Patrick called out from the back every time the door chimed, offering a cheery hello that every customer returned with a hearty grin.

A girl behind the counter pushed a button and the scent of freshly ground coffee beans filled the air.

Todd cleared his throat.

Sam sipped her coffee and lifted her eyebrows at Callie.

"How long have you known about this?" Todd voiced the question amid a chorus of laughter from a group of teenagers tucked into a booth in the corner. A girl tossed an empty wrapper at the boy across from her.

Ah, teenage love. She remembered those days. Sitting across from Brody and laughing with their friends. Tension knotted her muscles.

"Callie. How long?" Todd's tone brooked no sort of argument.

Callie inhaled through her nose and slowly let it leave out her mouth. "Since Texas."

"Why am I just now hearing about this?"

"I thought we could keep running."

"You can't ride a blind horse." Todd huffed. Through the phone, Callie heard his chair squeak. "You'll ride Maverick for the stampede. Glow's no longer on your string."

Her string. Right. Glow was the only horse she'd ever ridden during a rodeo until last week. Callie pressed her back into the padded booth, letting the sensation ground her. "I think she can still race, Todd. Brody has been training her, and she's coming along."

"The risk of liability is too high. We can't let you in the arena on a blind mount."

"The only person at risk is me."

"And your contract says that you're our responsibility." He breathed heavily through the phone and Callie knew she'd not like what he had to say next. "Maybe it's time we took another look at your contract. You're due for renewal in a month."

"You're pushing me out?" Incredulous, Callie almost dropped the phone.

Sam's eyebrows shot to her hairline. If Todd wanted Callie out, would Sam be next?

"That should be my decision. Not yours." She wanted out of the circuit. She'd told Brody this would be her last ride. What if Brody didn't want her to come back home after she'd lied about Glow and her finances? Where were her dreams leading her if not back to Tamarack Springs?

"You're not giving us much choice unless you're willing to use a different horse. Every time we bring it up, you're set against any horse that isn't Glow. Someone has to give, and it won't be the company." He waited, but Callie had no words to answer. "We'll see you in Kentucky. Get there in time to practice with Maverick."

Todd hung up, leaving Callie's ears ringing.

"Okay, now I feel bad." Sam winced and propped her chin in her hands. "I thought he'd take it better than that."

"Don't bother. We both know how this ends." Callie stared out the front window, watching as Tamarack Springs unwound across the sidewalk. Bells chimed from the coffee shop's front door and another rush of teenagers hurried in. A family of four stopped at the ice cream shop across the street, the father holding the door open for his wife and kids. Callie's throat ached at holding back tears. "What a rotten set of options. Either I ride Maverick or I risk violating my contract by refusing."

Sam made a point to look out the window. "Charming little town. I can see the draw of coming back. 'Course, that cowboy back at the ranch doesn't hurt." She winked and flashed a mischievous grin.

Yeah. If Brody ever talked to Callie again.

Sam's smile faded. "You said you were thinking about quitting after this season." Sam sighed. "Why not ride Maverick, then call it quits?"

Was she being too unyielding by wanting to finish her career on Glow? It made perfect sense when she'd first brought Glow home, but now her thoughts jumbled and refused to sort themselves into anything resembling a coherent path.

"Look, Callie." Sam sipped her espresso and then folded her hands on top of the table. "I have no need for another horse. Glow has always been yours to ride. You were the best rider out there. It made things more exciting to go up against you. I don't want to take Glow away from you, but I can't just let her go for nothing. I'm no saint, but I like to think that I helped you out."

Right. Helped her straight into a contract. That was Callie's own fault for not reading every word. "What do you suggest?" Her own coffee soured in her stomach.

"I guess you'll have to win the stampede." Sam scrunched her nose. Her lilac perfume drifted when the front door opened and let in a gust of hot air. "I'll give you Glow back for the same price I paid for her."

Callie's tension melted. A reasonable price. If she won at the stampede, she could buy Glow. Then what? Her future stretched into the distance, a blank canvas. She'd spent her life running in circles. Time to head straight and see where she ended up. "Thanks, Sam." She tapped her toes on the cracked floor and picked up her coffee cup.

One problem down.

All she had to do now was face Brody's wrath.

Sam drove Callie back to the ranch and dropped her off at the barn.

Brody met her at the doors, holding Glow's halter and lead. "I can't do this, Callie."

The words held a world of hurt. Ten years' worth and all the betrayals in between. She'd done it again, made promises she couldn't keep. "Brody—"

"Don't." He held up a hand and shoved the gear in her direction. "Please don't try and explain. You lied to me. You've been lying to everyone—yourself most of all. You said you want to give up the rodeo, but every time you have the chance, you run right back."

"This is the last one." She'd felt a moment of devastation when Todd mentioned her contract, followed by a rush of relief. It was time to end it. "I'm coming back."

He shook his head. "The uncertainty is too much for me. I can't fall in love with you again. There are not enough pieces left of me for you to run off and take them with you." Shadows filled his eyes, his voice wavering from its tight baritone.

Callie put her hands on his shoulders and held on. "I'm coming back. And I'll bring all your pieces with me. I'm not leaving you because of the rodeo. I need this. For me. For Glow." She pressed her lips to his and lingered over the familiar rush that his touch brought.

She stepped back, her gaze searching his. "I'm leaving for Kentucky."

It was the wrong thing to say. Brody removed his hands from her hips and pushed away like she'd burned him. He dropped the halter at her feet. The lead followed. Hot pink contrasted against the grass and her worn boots.

"I'm coming back." She whispered the words at Brody's broad back.

He hunched his shoulders but kept walking.

Chapter Fourteen

Callie missed Brody and the rest of his family to the point that she stopped eating. Every bite made her sick. Dark circles ringed her eyes from sleepless nights. She'd texted Tenley and Molly, asking about the family, and received replies that all was well. At least they were still talking to her.

She couldn't ask specifically about Brody. They all knew. They must. His family was too close not to figure out what had happened.

Leaving the first time had been hard, but this time... Callie hefted the saddle from Glow's back and gripped the leather until her fingers cramped. Their practice run this morning had proved one thing. Brody was right. Glow wasn't ready.

I'm sorry, Lord. Sorry I failed You, and sorry for the misdirection I allowed by not revealing Glow's blindness. Please let Brody hear me out when I go home.

The barn manager tipped his hat and took Glow's reins. "Morning, Miss Callie. Want me to take Glow to her stall? Todd's waiting for you."

In other words, she had no choice but to let the man

take Glow. The familiar sights and smells of the Rockford Stables washed over her. After leaving the ranch behind, this place had become home. Or as close as any place ever did.

Hay fluttered over the concrete floor, blown one way then the other by the overhead fans that kept the sweltering heat at bay. Riders chattered from every available space. Half were here for the stampede, the Rockford Stables home to many during these events.

"You okay?" Sam stuck her head out from her horse's stall. Seeing Callie's expression, she moved closer and dropped her voice. "You sure this is what you want?"

Was she? She'd lost track of what she wanted. Working with Brody again had messed with her head. She'd been happy here, riding the circuit with Rockford footing her expenses. Winning belt buckles on occasion and living the rodeo life. She loved it here. Didn't she? No. Not anymore. This place no longer made her eyes shine and her heart trip. One more rodeo. Blowing hair from her forehead, Callie nodded. "I'm good. I should go see what Todd wants."

She kept her pace slow down the barn aisle to keep from scaring the horses. Todd's office was in the main building, across from the barn and up the stairs. The wooden steps creaked under her boots. Callie hesitated outside the door and pressed a hand to her heart, attempting to ease the beat.

Lifting her chin, she rapped her knuckles on the door and waited for Todd to call out before she entered and dropped into the upholstered chair. The wooden desk separated them by four feet, but even from there, Callie could feel Todd's displeasure.

She leaned forward and planted her elbows on her

knees. "What can I do to convince you to let me run on Glow?"

"Nothing." Todd laced his fingers together atop the desk. Frames lined the wall behind his head.

Photos of previous barrel racers stared back at Callie. An image of her on Glow during a ride in Tucson rested on the far right. Glow's perfect form bent around the barrel. Callie's expression showed her hunger for the win. Mouth twisted, hand tight on the saddle. They'd won that day, the biggest purse she'd ever claimed.

"I saw your practice run yesterday. And this morning. Glow hesitated on the trot and barely managed a lope away from the last barrel. We sponsor you because you can win." Todd pressed his fingers to his forehead. "Are you done? You've been slowing down for a while. Is that Glow getting old or are you ready to hang up your boots?"

"I'm not quitting the stampede." The idea of quitting seemed equal parts too easy and yet too complicated to contemplate. After this, she could walk away free and clear from the rigors of racing, hopefully take Glow, and do anything she wanted.

What did she want?

Callie eyed the portraits again and the old fire tempered. It lingered, flickering but not dead.

The need to go out on a high note, the longing to smell the arena dirt one last time before she walked away, pressed inside her.

"What if I did want out of my contract before the stampede?" An idea sparked, fueled by her past self staring back at her from the wall.

A pained expression crossed Todd's face. Gray hair lined his temples but his own rodeo past showed in the shiny belt buckle he still wore and the trophies tucked into the shelves on either side of the framed portraits. He'd been a bull rider in his younger years. Well-known and respected, he knew what it was like to be on the way out and needing one last ride to cinch the past before moving into a new future.

"I need this, Todd. One last ride on Glow. I don't care if we walk the barrels. We need this. I need to say goodbye in my own way. Glow and I started this career together. It's only fair we go out the same way. I understand you have a business to run. I don't want to hurt you in any way. I won't be renewing my contract. I'm done. Just let me have this one thing."

Todd leaned his head back and stared at the ceiling. The chair squeaked as he rocked.

Callie's heart raced.

One last rodeo.

Then what? Brody had let her walk away without a backward glance or a goodbye. They were forever stuck in this loop of being incapable of giving what the other needed.

The answer came quicker than lightning across the summer sky. She could change their pattern. Not every ride had to go right, left, left. The blank canvas of her future began filling in. She loved Brody. Then and now. Forever. Life with the rodeo had never fulfilled her need to prove herself because the people she wanted to love her already did.

Her parents were her parents, and their conditions had nothing to do with her. Winning every rodeo across the world wouldn't change how they felt. But the Jacobses? They never stopped treating her like a daughter. Accepted her as one of their own from the moment she'd returned.

Brody had helped her when he could have turned her away. When he should have told her to take a hike, he'd let her stay.

Tenley had offered Callie a place to live and Luke had made her remember how much she loved teaching.

That was it. Callie almost burst out laughing. She would teach kids to ride. Not just ride. Rodeo.

"Ride Maverick in the race, and I'll allow a special, nontimed event for you and Glow to say your farewell." Todd's voice snapped her from her revelation. He sounded defeated, but his eyes shone. His lips quirked up into a tired smile. "Give 'em a ride they'll remember forever."

It took every effort not to leap from the chair, toss her hat into the air and whoop. Callie managed a demure nod.

Todd's face cracked into a broad smile. "Go live a good life, Callie. We'll miss you."

She threw out a hand and pumped his, gripping it between her palms. "Thank you."

"You come across any talent, you'll send them my way?"

"Sure," Callie called over her shoulder and bolted down the steps. She'd done it. It wasn't the ride she'd envisioned, but it would be enough.

Two days later, Callie stood outside the arena, tucked into the shadows of the barn with her shoulders against the wall as riders rode back and forth on their way to their competitions. Barrel racing was next, and Sam was the first rider of the day.

Callie pushed her hands into her pockets to keep from chewing her nails. The announcer's voice rang out over the loudspeakers, announcing Sam's time. She'd be the one to beat.

Sam trotted down the alley and Callie held up her hand for a high five. Sam slapped Callie's palm as she passed. "Beat that."

"Oh, I plan to." Callie shot her routine response at Sam's back and leaned over to watch the next rider bolt down the alley and around the first barrel. Shouts erupted from the crowd when the barrel rocked. They heaved a collective sigh when it stayed upright.

Maverick nosed Callie's neck, blowing warm breath down her collar. Callie faced the pinto gelding and ran a hand across the white star in the center of his forehead. "You and me, buddy. Let's give them something to talk about."

She mounted up as her name was called. Cheers rang out from the bleachers. Nerves tickled her stomach, the all-consuming butterflies sprouting a thousand wings. Callie checked her stirrups and shook her head at the man ready to walk her down the alley. Maverick wasn't one to bolt into the arena. He preferred a quieter approach that was no less volatile.

They trotted into the arena. Blue barrels set in a perfect triangle awaited them. Callie eyed the dirt, looking for anything that might trip Maverick. She turned him in a circle and gave him a squeeze. She was ready.

Maverick snorted and shot forward, his powerful muscles launching them across the arena and around the first barrel before Callie had pulled in a solid breath. *Whoa.* He flew around the second barrel and faced the third, his speed whipping hair around her face, giving Callie his all as they took the turn and headed home. They flashed past the timer and Callie tugged on the reins.

Maverick tossed his head and slowed to a trot. Callie

glanced at the clock, the crowd's roar telling her more than the flashing numbers. They'd beat Sam.

The gelding had the power to be faster than any horse Callie had ever ridden. Whoever came behind her to be his rider was in for a treat. He loved to run. Even now, he pranced, head high.

She walked Maverick from the arena, chin lifted and a smile pulling at her cheeks. The crowd continued to cheer. Many stood and stomped their feet. Flags billowed in the breeze and brought the rodeo arena smells swirling into the air.

Leather creaked as she gave Maverick a bit of rein. The gelding trotted toward his stall. Tomorrow, he'd be loaded up in Todd's trailer and hauled to the next rodeo.

"Nice run."

Callie spun Maverick to face the voice she could never forget.

Brody stood at the doorway to the barn, arms crossed and grin spread wide.

Maverick tossed his head. Callie dropped from the saddle and wobbled at the sight of Brody. Maverick nosed her, his whiskers tickling her cheek. She nudged him away. "You came."

"I had an enlightening conversation with my sister."

"Molly?"

He shook his head and grinned wider. "Tenley. She said, in no uncertain terms, that I was a fool. An idiot. She didn't know how I'd managed to survive this long because I lacked the brain capacity of an ant."

Laughter slipped out. Callie held her stomach and pressed her lips together.

Brody closed the distance. "I messed up. Big-time. I decided a long time ago that you didn't need me. Until you did, I thought I couldn't love you. And I refused to need you." He cupped her cheek in his calloused palm. "I was wrong. I've always needed you. And those pieces of my heart that you took? I don't want them back. They're yours. Now and forever."

Warm tears rained down her cheeks. She sniffed and dabbed her nose. Words failed her. Seeing him here wrenched open a chasm of emotion.

Brody produced a clean handkerchief from his pocket and handed it to her. His shoulders lifted and his eyes gleamed under his Stetson. "You want to win this?"

"I think I already have." Callie couldn't resist adding a little swagger to her step when they turned and navigated toward the stalls again.

Brody held out a manila envelope.

"What's this?"

"Well, if you'll read it, then you'll see for yourself." He took Maverick's reins and led the gelding toward the stables.

Callie pulled out a sheaf of papers and scanned the documents. She made it to the end then started back at the beginning. "Brody." She shoved the papers at him. "Does this say what I think it does?"

"That depends. Do you think that it says you have special permission from the rodeo to ride two horses in this one-time event?" Brody removed Maverick's tack and stepped out of the stall.

"But Todd already agreed." She waved the papers and frowned until her cheeks ached.

"Todd agreed to let you *walk* Glow around the barrels like some decrepit pony on its last legs. This gives you a real chance to walk away with the win. On Glow."

Brody had a look in his eyes that sent a jolt straight to her heart. He was doing it again, tackling her hurdles.

How had he known? And, more importantly… "How did you do this?" The words stuttered out between breaths. She dashed a tear away before it could run down her cheek and scanned the barn. No one paid them any attention. The riders were too busy warming up their mounts or razzing each other over their times.

Brody leaned his hip on the stall door and rubbed Maverick's forehead. "I talked to Sam. All the riders agreed. They want to see what a blind horse can do. Like you said, you already have the time to beat." He paused and then smiled her absolute favorite smile, the one that pulled wrinkles into the corners of his eyes. He leaned in close, his breath fanning her cheek. "So go beat it."

He turned away.

Callie snagged the sleeve of his Western snap-button shirt and pulled him to a stop. "I can't do this without you, Brody. I think…" She paused and swallowed the knot in her throat. "What if we fail? What if we get out there and she refuses to run?"

"But what if she flies around those barrels like she has wings?"

What if? The possibility was too much to hope for, but why not try?

"Trust her." Brody's hands landed on her shoulders. He held her tight, grounding her to the moment.

She breathed in through her nose, hauling in the smells so familiar to her that she almost didn't even smell them at all. Funnel cakes. Dirt. Sweat. Horse.

And Brody. Dear, wonderful Brody. He burned through her defenses and set the world alight.

Trust her horse. Trust in God. Trust that they'd make it through.

Callie dipped her head into a nod. "Let's take it home." She threw her arms around Brody and squeezed. "Thank you." The words were too small for what she felt, but they were all she could offer. At least for now. Shouting "I love you" seemed a little awkward right here in the middle of the barn. Then again. Wait. An idea sparked and burned brighter by the second.

"Hey, Callie, your second run is coming up. Better get ready." Max rode past on his horse Blaze.

Callie grabbed Brody's hand and hauled him toward Glow's stall. The mare weaved from side to side, head low and sides heaving. Her ears swiveled, no doubt trying to catch all the sounds and find something familiar. She knew this place, but being unable to see it seemed to be overwhelming her.

Brody hooked his thumbs into his jeans and whistled. "This is going to take a minute." He grabbed a lead rope and hooked it onto Glow's halter. "Where do you tack her up?"

"Over here." Callie led him to a quiet corner and rushed back for her tack. By the time she returned, Brody had brushed Glow down and cleaned out her hooves.

Glow relaxed, one muscle at a time, under Brody's steady hands. "Is your heart racing right now?"

His question sent her heart skipping. She ran a palm over it and bit her lip. "I think there's a hummingbird living in there."

"As long as it's from excitement, we're good to go." Brody's voice held that steady cadence. It eased through the air like warm molasses. Everything it touched turned sweet and golden.

Callie took a deep breath and moved to Glow's side. She trailed her hand over the mare's withers, up through her mane and then to her forelock.

Brody moved back and let Callie step in front of Glow. She bracketed the mare's jaws in her hands and lifted her head until they were eye to eye. Glow blinked. Her sightless eyes moved, and Callie's breath hitched. She leaned forward until their foreheads touched. "I've pushed for this for weeks. And now that it's here, all I can think is that I never took you into consideration."

Tears burned in the back of her throat. "Brody has done a wonderful thing, Glow, but I need to know that you're okay with this." It wasn't like the horse could answer her, but Callie waited. She trusted Glow, thanks to Brody, but did the horse trust her?

Brody lingered beside Glow and Callie while the two took a moment to compose themselves. They could do this. They only had to believe and trust in each other. Not an easy task, especially after their last few months.

Finally, Callie lifted her head. Tears glimmered in her eyes.

Brody's throat tightened. Was she about to say they couldn't do it?

She took the saddle pad and tossed it over Glow's back. "We're going to win this. And when we do, I'll buy you back from Sam." She glanced over her shoulder.

A jolt ran through Brody at the mention of Sam. That was one problem he'd been unable to solve after sending Callie away. He'd been a fool to push her into leaving. Glow deserved better, and so did Callie. He'd failed them by allowing his anger and fear to reign over him. He let the pride he felt for Callie carry in his voice. "You've already won."

He'd never let his fear take over. Never again. Once this was done, he'd tell her how he felt.

She looked ready to argue when the speakers squawked.

"Callie Wade to the warm-up ring." The announcer's voice rang out across the barn.

Callie jerked her head in the direction of the arena. Her throat dipped in a hard swallow. "That's my warning call. We'll have just enough time to warm up." She made quick work of the saddle and bridle then swung aboard. "Come with me?"

Brody nodded, barely managing to keep his smile at bay. It had taken a lot of thought and prayers to convince him to make the trek to Kentucky. Even if Callie walked away without riding, coming to see her had been worth every mile and every dollar spent. He walked alongside Callie as she maneuvered the mare down the long barn aisle and out into a covered arena.

Two other riders circled the perimeter.

Callie hesitated and gathered up her reins. She looked down and her gaze locked with his. "No matter what happens, thank you for everything. You gave me back a piece of myself that I didn't know I'd been missing." She urged Glow into the arena before he could respond.

He didn't mind. Later. Everything would come together later. Right now, all he wanted was to see the woman he loved ride Glow with the ease and grace that made spectators hold their breath at the beauty they created.

Glow stretched her head out and shook her mane. Her stride went from quick and clipped to languid. She appeared to be enjoying herself.

Callie asked for a trot. Glow picked up the pace, bouncing Callie in the saddle for the first few steps until she settled.

The overhead speaker crackled. "Dean Smith."

The male rider in the arena with Callie moved to the gate. Not long now.

Seconds later, cheers erupted from the crowd. The sound pulsed in Brody's ears. Had the man beaten Callie and Maverick's time? Brody had done his best to help Callie. She was allowed two runs, but only her time on Maverick counted toward the win.

This run on Glow was sentimental, but he desperately wanted Callie to have the best run of her life.

With another crackle, the announcer called for the last rider before Callie. They were alone in the exercise arena. Glow's hooves threw clods of dirt into the air.

Callie grimaced and slowed her to a walk. "She's resisting."

"Take her to the far side of the arena." Brody slung his body between the rails and straightened. He gave Glow a critical once-over. "Do you trust me?" His voice carried across the yards of dirt.

Glow raised her head and pricked her ears. She remembered this game. His heart slowed when Glow pawed the dirt.

Callie nodded so hard, her hat wobbled and almost fell. "I trust you."

"Come to me." He whistled at the same time Callie leaned low in the saddle.

Glow dug her hooves in and launched like she'd been shot from a cannon. Her sides heaved and she gained speed with every stride.

"Turn." Callie patted Glow's shoulder then grabbed

the horn. She leaned and Glow turned. Callie's boot brushed across Brody's back from the tightness of the turn. "Run home, Glow." Callie chirruped and relaxed the reins.

Glow tucked into the turn and gathered her haunches, then she was gone, racing across the arena faster than he'd ever seen her run.

Callie sat back in the saddle and Glow slid into a perfect stop. Callie whooped and threw her arms around Glow's neck. What a great practice run.

They were about to make history.

Brody took up his place beside Callie's stirrup and they walked toward the main arena in time to see the previous woman's time flash. He glanced at the leaderboard. Callie and Maverick still had the top spot.

Callie followed his eyes and a smile broke out that shone brighter than the sunlight filtering into the arena. The crowd rose to its feet when Callie and Glow appeared.

"This is all for you and Glow. Show them what it's like to have fun." He patted Callie's booted foot and stepped back.

Callie dipped her chin and gathered up the reins. Glow began to prance. Her ears perked up and she snorted when the crowd stamped its feet and clapped. A chant began on Brody's left. "Gol-den Glow. Gol-den Glow." They stomped on each syllable and the chant picked up speed.

"They're calling for you." Callie ran her hands up and down Glow's neck. She spun her head to face Brody. "Thank you."

Glow's speed shot them into the arena and around the first barrel.

Brody held his breath at the beauty of the perfect turn. Glow wheeled and cut left. Her shoulder brushed the barrel. It rocked and the crowd gasped, but the barrel didn't fall. Callie never looked back. Glow raced like the wind itself carried her. They ran for the third barrel and then they were running toward him.

He'd never seen anything more beautiful than the woman he loved smiling fit to rival the sun as she ran to him astride her favorite horse.

Dirt sprayed as Glow slid into another perfect stop. All the fear and uncertainty disappeared in that run. They were a team again. Callie jumped from the saddle and leaped into his arms.

Brody looked over her head and blinked at the time. Faster. She'd beaten her time on Maverick. Glow had an undisputed claim on the rodeo's record. The entire arena held its breath. Callie held tight to his neck. "I love you, Brody. Give me five minutes to say goodbye, and you'll never see me walk away again." She didn't even look at the board to see her time.

She left him speechless. He'd always wondered what *gobsmacked* meant. Now he knew. He felt it, a lingering pinch of hope that tied him in knots and left him reeling.

Callie mounted Glow and trotted to the center of the ring. She held out her hand and a man in a string tie and black Stetson ran a microphone out to her. The crowd muttered, confusion showing on many faces.

Brody focused on Callie. She was the only one who mattered to him.

"I'd like to thank my sponsors and my fellow riders for allowing this today." Callie gestured toward Glow and then at the time still flashing in bold red strokes. She locked onto Brody. Her hand tightened on the microphone. "I'd also like to thank a very special man, who's here with us today."

The crowd began peering around, their feet creating resounding creaks and groans as they shifted and searched.

"I have a short story to tell then I'll get out of your way and let you get back to your rodeo."

That got their attention. Even the wind stopped blowing as Callie sat atop Glow like a queen addressing her court. "This horse I'm riding, Golden Glow, many of you know her. You cheered for her when she came into the ring. What you don't know is that she's blind."

The crowd gasped then fell silent. A baby cried and was quickly shushed.

"For the last several weeks, I've been working with a great trainer. He's a wonderful man *and*—" she smiled "—the love of my life." She waved at him, beckoning for Brody to join her. "Brody, get out here. Ladies and gentlemen, may I present Brody Jacobs of Triple Bar Ranch. Without him, Glow and I would have never been able to make this run today."

Roars filled Brody's ears. Callie loved him. He ran across the sand to her side. "I love you, Callie Wade." He kissed her then, giving his whole heart to the woman who held him captive.

Callie was breathless when they separated. "I should hope so." Her smile bloomed even brighter. "Let's go home."

Epilogue

Six months later

Callie called out encouragement as Amanda and Beauty—her two newest students—trotted around the arena. The same covered ring where the fundraiser rodeo had taken place was now her training ground.

Beauty snorted, and Amanda laughed when the white mare shook her mane. "I think she's excited." Amanda patted the arched neck. "Can we trot over the poles now?"

"Sure. Go around one more time, then line her up and head across." The poles were nothing more than pool noodles spaced out across the middle of the arena. Callie hoped the exercise would teach horse and rider patience and help their balance as they maneuvered over obstacles.

They completed the first pass without touching a single pole. Amanda stopped the mare and flung her arms around the horse's neck. "I love you." The mare bobbed her head as though in answer.

"Okay. Take her on into the barn and get her tack off." Callie waved the pair away. Four months she'd been teaching here at Daniel Wells's barn. She loved every minute.

Brody sauntered to the railing and pushed his Stetson up. Blue eyes caught the light and sent shivers down her arms. Goose bumps erupted. Six months since she'd given up the rodeo and come home. "About done for the day?"

She nodded and gathered up her notebook and phone from the bleachers. "How's the gelding?"

"Coming along. Hope to have a saddle on him by the end of the month."

Daniel had been a blessing to them both. He and Brody had compromised. Daniel sent clients to Brody when he could, and Brody trained at the Wellses' stable two days a week. Daniel gave Callie a job teaching younger students, and her winnings from the rodeo had been enough to purchase Glow's shares from Sam.

Tenley had given them the final numbers for the fundraiser, and the medical bills were paid in full. She'd also admitted she was studying to get her certification in equine therapy and hoped to start bringing in kids and horses in the fall.

Even Brody couldn't argue with Tenley's hope for her future.

Callie had never seen Brody as shocked as he was the day when he'd realized he was now truly working for himself and his own dreams. That had turned out to be staying right where he was on the ranch.

"Can you take a look at something before we go?" Brody put an arm around her shoulders and pulled her into his side.

The move brought their hips together and Callie adjusted her steps so they moved in sync. "Sure. What's up?"

"There's a mare in the broodmare barn I want you to look at." His tone was bright, but a pinch of tension shot through Callie.

"Is there a problem?"

"No." He winked at her and urged her faster. "Trust me, this is a good thing."

Then why was he pulling her? Callie shuffled her boots to keep up. They scurried into the barn. Glow stood in the crossties, wearing a neon-pink halter. Bows lined her mane and a bell dangled from her chin. "What's this?"

"Check her out. Tell me what you think." Brody stuck his thumbs in his pockets and shot her a smile. "There's a note tied to the bell."

Callie hesitated before moving to Glow and untying the note. Glow nosed her side and set the bell to jingling. What was her horse doing in this barn? She unfolded the note and read quickly. When she finished, she spun to face Brody.

He grinned and dropped to a knee while extracting a box from his pocket. "Callie Wade, I have loved you for as long as I can remember. I nearly lost myself when you left. Both times." He winked to soften his words. "I want to spend the rest of my life with you by my side. Will you marry me?"

The note fluttered to the concrete floor. Callie's hands covered her mouth. A tiny squeak emerged. Glow whinnied her obvious approval.

"Is that a yes?" Brody laughed and jiggled the box. "Do you know how hard concrete is when all your weight is on one knee?"

"Then get up and put that ring on me." She dropped

one hand and wiggled her fingers at him. Her heart filled to overflowing at the sight of Brody's proposal. The ring glinted. Callie gasped. "Is that the same ring?"

Ten years ago, he'd proposed in the heat of the moment in the hope of getting her to stay. The fact that he'd kept the ring all these years brought her to tears.

His Adam's apple bobbed. "I couldn't get rid of it. Never understood why until the day you drove back into my life." He slid the ring onto her finger and kissed her knuckles. "You're not getting away this time. You can ride as far as you want. I'll always be right behind you."

"Why not stay beside me?" She stood on tiptoes and kissed him. When she dropped back down, she wiggled her eyebrows and chuckled. "No more rodeos for me, cowboy. I've had my fill of running. Wherever you are, that's where I want to be."

She ran her arms around his waist and squeezed. "Now, explain that note and tell me why my horse is here."

Brody launched into a detailed plan for teaching Glow how to navigate her blindness. "She's learned to trust you. Now I think it might be a good idea to find a horse that you can turn her out into the fields with. That's where the bell comes in. Being blind means she has to trust her other senses. Trust her instincts. Once we find the right companion, we'll put the bell on them so Glow will always know where they are."

Blind trust. They could all learn something from the plucky mare who refused to let the loss of her sight keep her hostage.

Callie had learned her lesson. Love for Brody filled her to bursting. She'd given him her trust, and her heart, without hope of ever getting them back. He treated them as pieces of himself and treasured her every day. This next step was as natural as breathing.

* * * * *

If you liked this story from Tabitha Bouldin,
check out these previous Love Inspired books:

The Cowgirl's Sacrifice *by Tina Radcliffe*
A Christmas Bargain *by Mindy Obenhaus*
Journey to Forgiveness *by Danica Favorite*

Available now from Love Inspired!
Find more great reads at www.LoveInspired.com.

Dear Reader,

Thank you for taking the time to read Brody and Callie's story. Writing for Love Inspired has been a long-awaited dream come true. God knew what He was doing when He told me to wait. He taught me patience.

Like Callie, I have a passion for horses, and rescuing a blind quarter horse while in the process of writing this story brought home the truth of second chances that Callie desperately wanted for herself. I think there are times when we all want to start over or to be given the chance to prove that we're not the same person we used to be.

Staying connected with readers is another thing that brings me joy. I hope you'll check out my website at tabithabouldin.com, where you can sign up for my newsletter or follow me on my socials.

Tabitha Bouldin

COMING NEXT MONTH FROM
Love Inspired

AN AMISH MOTHER FOR HIS CHILD
Amish Country Matches • by Patricia Johns

After giving up on romance, Verna Kauffman thought a marriage of convenience would give her everything she's longed for—a family. But marrying reserved Adam Lantz comes with a list of rules Verna wasn't expecting. Can they overcome their differences to discover that all they really need is each other?

HER SCANDALOUS AMISH SECRET
by Jocelyn McClay

A life-changing event propels Lydia Troyer to return to her Amish community to repair her damaged reputation—with a baby in tow. And when she finds old love Jonah Lapp working on her family home, she knows winning back his trust will be hardest of all...especially once she reveals her secret.

FINDING THEIR WAY BACK
K-9 Companions • by Jenna Mindel

Twenty-eight years ago, Erica Laine and Ben Fisher were engaged to be married...until Erica broke his heart. Now, as they work together on a home that Erica needs to fulfill her new role as a traveling nurse, their past connection is rekindled. But can love take root when Erica is committed to leaving again?

FOR THE SAKE OF HER SONS
True North Springs • by Allie Pleiter

Following a tragedy, Willa Scottson doesn't hold much hope for healing while at Camp True North Springs. But swim instructor Bruce Lawrence is determined to help the grieving widow and her twin boys. This is his chance to make amends—if Willa will let him once the truth comes out...

THE GUARDIAN AGREEMENT
by Lorraine Beatty

When jilted bride Olivia Marshall is forced to work with her ex-fiancé, Ben Kincaid, it stirs up old pain. Yet she finds herself asking Ben for help when her four-year-old nephew is abandoned on her doorstep. Will their truce lead to a second chance...or will Ben's past stand in their way?

SAVING THE SINGLE DAD'S BOOKSTORE
by Nicole Lam

Inheriting his grandfather's bookstore forces Dominic Tang to return to his hometown faced with a big decision—keep it or sell. But manager Gianna Marchesi insists she can prove the business's worth. Then an accident leads to expensive damages, making Dominic choose between risking everything or following his heart...

LICNM1123

HARLEQUIN
PLUS

Try the best multimedia subscription service for romance readers like you!

Read, Watch and Play.

Experience the easiest way to get the romance content you crave.

Start your **FREE TRIAL** at
<u>www.harlequinplus.com/freetrial</u>.